Y0-BUD-988

Triangle

By Danielle Steel

TRIANGLE · JOY · RESURRECTION · ONLY THE BRAVE
NEVER TOO LATE · UPSIDE DOWN · THE BALL AT VERSAILLES · SECOND ACT
HAPPINESS · PALAZZO · THE WEDDING PLANNER · WORTHY OPPONENTS
WITHOUT A TRACE · THE WHITTIERS · THE HIGH NOTES · THE CHALLENGE
SUSPECTS · BEAUTIFUL · HIGH STAKES · INVISIBLE · FLYING ANGELS · THE BUTLER
COMPLICATIONS · NINE LIVES · FINDING ASHLEY · THE AFFAIR · NEIGHBORS
ALL THAT GLITTERS · ROYAL · DADDY'S GIRLS · THE WEDDING DRESS
THE NUMBERS GAME · MORAL COMPASS · SPY · CHILD'S PLAY · THE DARK SIDE
LOST AND FOUND · BLESSING IN DISGUISE · SILENT NIGHT · TURNING POINT
BEAUCHAMP HALL · IN HIS FATHER'S FOOTSTEPS · THE GOOD FIGHT · THE CAST
ACCIDENTAL HEROES · FALL FROM GRACE · PAST PERFECT · FAIRYTALE
THE RIGHT TIME · THE DUCHESS · AGAINST ALL ODDS · DANGEROUS GAMES
THE MISTRESS · THE AWARD · RUSHING WATERS · MAGIC · THE APARTMENT
PROPERTY OF A NOBLEWOMAN · BLUE · PRECIOUS GIFTS · UNDERCOVER
COUNTRY · PRODIGAL SON · PEGASUS · A PERFECT LIFE · POWER PLAY · WINNERS
FIRST SIGHT · UNTIL THE END OF TIME · THE SINS OF THE MOTHER
FRIENDS FOREVER · BETRAYAL · HOTEL VENDÔME · HAPPY BIRTHDAY
44 CHARLES STREET · LEGACY · FAMILY TIES · BIG GIRL · SOUTHERN LIGHTS
MATTERS OF THE HEART · ONE DAY AT A TIME · A GOOD WOMAN · ROGUE
HONOR THYSELF · AMAZING GRACE · BUNGALOW 2 · SISTERS · H.R.H.
COMING OUT · THE HOUSE · TOXIC BACHELORS · MIRACLE · IMPOSSIBLE · ECHOES
SECOND CHANCE · RANSOM · SAFE HARBOUR · JOHNNY ANGEL · DATING GAME
ANSWERED PRAYERS · SUNSET IN ST. TROPEZ · THE COTTAGE · THE KISS
LEAP OF FAITH · LONE EAGLE · JOURNEY · THE HOUSE ON HOPE STREET
THE WEDDING · IRRESISTIBLE FORCES · GRANNY DAN · BITTERSWEET
MIRROR IMAGE · THE KLONE AND I · THE LONG ROAD HOME · THE GHOST
SPECIAL DELIVERY · THE RANCH · SILENT HONOR · MALICE · FIVE DAYS IN PARIS
LIGHTNING · WINGS · THE GIFT · ACCIDENT · VANISHED · MIXED BLESSINGS
JEWELS · NO GREATER LOVE · HEARTBEAT · MESSAGE FROM NAM · DADDY · STAR
ZOYA · KALEIDOSCOPE · FINE THINGS · WANDERLUST · SECRETS · FAMILY ALBUM
FULL CIRCLE · CHANGES · THURSTON HOUSE · CROSSINGS · ONCE IN A LIFETIME
A PERFECT STRANGER · REMEMBRANCE · PALOMINO · LOVE: *POEMS* · THE RING
LOVING · TO LOVE AGAIN · SUMMER'S END · SEASON OF PASSION · THE PROMISE
NOW AND FOREVER · PASSION'S PROMISE · GOING HOME

Nonfiction

EXPECT A MIRACLE: *Quotations to Live and Love By*
PURE JOY: *The Dogs We Love*
A GIFT OF HOPE: *Helping the Homeless*
HIS BRIGHT LIGHT: *The Story of Nick Traina*

For Children

PRETTY MINNIE IN PARIS · PRETTY MINNIE IN HOLLYWOOD

DANIELLE STEEL

Triangle

A Novel

Delacorte Press | New York

Published in the United States by Delacorte Press,
an imprint of Random House,
a division of Penguin Random House LLC, New York.

Delacorte Press is a registered trademark and the DP colophon is
a trademark of Penguin Random House LLC.

Library of Congress Cataloging-in-Publication Data
Names: Steel, Danielle, author.
Title: Triangle : a novel / Danielle Steel.
Description: New York : Delacorte Press, 2024.
Identifiers: LCCN 2023034723 (print) | LCCN 2023034724 (ebook) |
ISBN 9780593498552 (hardcover ; acid-free paper) |
ISBN 9780593498569 (ebook)
Subjects: LCGFT: Novels.
Classification: LCC PS3569.T33828 T75 2024 (print) |
LCC PS3569.T33828 (ebook) | DDC 813/.54--dc23/eng/20230825
LC record available at https://lccn.loc.gov/2023034723
LC ebook record available at https://lccn.loc.gov/2023034724

Printed in the United States of America on acid-free paper

randomhousebooks.com

1st Printing

First Edition

To my beloved children,
Beatrix, Trevor, Todd,
Nick, Samantha, Victoria,
Vanessa, Maxx, and Zara,

May you find the right person and the right path,
and have a beautiful shared life,
however you choose to live it,
with honor, honesty, courage, and joy.

May you be blessed with many blessings
and endless happiness, always.
With all my heart and love forever,
                    Mom/D.S.

Triangle

Chapter 1

If anyone had asked small, delicate, beautiful blond Amanda Delanoe, she would have said she had the perfect life. She had a stylish look, a kind of natural chic which was partially inherited from both her parents, and she also had her own talent for giving everything she touched a special, very individual twist. She had an eye for beauty, fashion, and art, due to the milieu she had grown up in. Her father, Armand Delanoe, had a gift for business and fashion, and had started several very successful luxury brands, then acquired other established but failing companies and breathed new life into them. He had a talent for hiring the right people to bring his visions to fruition.

Amanda's mother, Felicia Farr, had been a famous model. Armand had fallen in love with her the first time he saw her on the runway at the fashion show of one of his brands. They married soon after. She was American and had the same striking blond looks as their daughter, although Felicia was tall and willowy. She had retired soon after Amanda was born, content to be Armand's wife and give up her modeling career. She had an elegant, classic style and became a showcase for many of the brands he owned by wearing their clothes to important social events and being photographed in them. Amanda's taste was more unusual and more personal. She had her father's eye for new fashions, but had chosen art as her career.

At thirty-nine, Amanda had an apartment she loved on the Left Bank in Paris, with a terrace that gave her a front-row seat to view the Eiffel Tower. The apartment reflected her eclectic taste, her travels, and her many passions. She had an important collection of contemporary art, and was part owner of a contemporary art gallery, Galerie Delanoe, which represented several well-known artists and a number of new unknowns whose careers she was shepherding carefully, with very satisfying results. She was a warm, caring person, who had been much loved as a child, and she lavished attention and affection on her artists. For now, they were her children, and they soaked up her generous praise like sponges. She never resented spending hours with her artists, listening to all their problems, and visiting them in their studios often to encourage them and see what new themes and techniques they were experimenting with. She was always willing to give advice or direction when asked.

Born in France, Amanda had also spent considerable time in the States and was a product of both cultures. She had the warm, passionate nature of the French and the cooler, more practical side of her American blood, plus a solid head for business, which her business partner, Pascal Leblanc, appreciated enormously. They were the perfect complement to each other. Pascal was more traditional in his training and outlook, and Amanda was more adventurous, willing to take a risk with an unknown artist. She had started the gallery herself in her twenties, and Pascal had joined her a year after she opened. It was a solid relationship and friendship, born of mutual respect.

Pascal was forty-four, five years older than Amanda. Neither of them was married, and their working relationship had never been confused or polluted by romantic overtones. They frequently gave each other advice of a personal nature. Amanda was given to serious relationships and spent long periods on her own between the men she loved, after the relationships failed for whatever reason.

Pascal's romances were brief and passionate. They rarely lasted more than a few months. There was always a new woman to fall madly in love with around the next corner. His relationships were like summer fireworks and burned out just as quickly. He had an aversion to the concept of marriage. It sounded like a prison sentence to him. It wasn't a goal for Amanda either. She didn't seek it but wasn't as opposed to it as Pascal. She had watched her parents' once happy marriage deteriorate and eventually implode, so she was cautious. And so far no one had made her feel that she wanted to be married, and children weren't a strong lure for her either. She was blissfully happy as she was, unattached for the moment, and happy with her friends, her work, and her dog.

Her education had been as evenly divided as her nationality. She had grown up in Paris until her parents divorced when she was twelve, and her mother took Amanda back to New York with her. It had been a big adjustment for Amanda, leaving France and going to an American school. Her father had always been her hero. She spent holidays and summers with him after the divorce and loved going back to France to be with him and her old friends.

Neither of her parents had ever precisely explained to her the reason for the divorce. She had been mildly aware of the dissent between them for a year or two, and saw some serious turbulence and angry fights. It was only later that she realized that her father's frequent infidelities had been the reason for it. He loved his wife, but he could never resist the beautiful women, mostly models, who crossed his path.

Her mother had been deeply unhappy when they left Paris. Armand visited Amanda frequently in New York, since he had business there. Her parents had divorced when Amanda was at an age when adolescence quickly took over, and in her early teen years, she and her mother argued more than they ever had before. Amanda was constantly at war with Felicia and blamed her for the divorce, since she couldn't imagine her father causing it, nor any reason for her mother leaving him. Felicia never told Amanda her reasons, out of respect for Armand. And Amanda was too young to know. Armand had taken responsibility for it, and tried to explain to Amanda that her mother wasn't entirely wrong, but she didn't believe him, and continued to blame her mother. And then, disaster struck. Armand had been generous with his ex-wife, mostly out of guilt, and Felicia had lived a very comfortable life. Amanda went to one of the best private schools in New York and they lived in a very pretty apartment. Felicia was on her way to a party in the Hamptons with friends on a helicopter they'd chartered when a flash storm hit, the helicopter crashed, and everyone on it was killed, including Amanda's mother. Amanda was at a friend's house for the weekend, and the friend's mother tearfully told Amanda what had happened.

Amanda was fourteen then. It was two years after she and her mother had left Paris. Her father arrived immediately to bring her home after the funeral in New York three days later. He was almost as devastated as his daughter at his ex-wife's death. Amanda was consumed with guilt about their teenage battles, and Armand for the many affairs he'd had, which had driven Felicia away and broken her heart. He took Amanda back to Paris, and lavished love on her. There was always a woman in his life and on his arm, rarely the same one for long, and he assured Amanda that she was the love of his life.

Amanda went back to her old school in Paris and lived with her father. She missed her mother fiercely, but she and Armand had a good life, and she never lacked for attention. She felt more French than ever when she went home. Until then she had always felt a little American in France and a little French in New York, and in fact, she was both. Maybe subconsciously, to maintain her tie to her mother, four years after her mother's death, Amanda decided to go to college in New York, and attended New York University, majoring in art history. She went back to France after she graduated. She enjoyed her college years, but also realized that culturally she was more French than American and was ready to go home. Her time in New York reminded her of her life with her mother, but she had grown up French, and Paris was home.

She had gotten a job at an excellent art gallery in Paris, and was thoroughly enjoying her life there, when disaster struck again. Her father fell gravely ill six months after she moved back. He was diagnosed with pancreatic cancer and was dead in five months. He was only sixty-two. It left Amanda alone in the world, without parents, grandparents, siblings, cousins or aunts and uncles, at twenty-two. But her father had also left her a sizable inheritance and had left his affairs in good order. He had partners in his businesses, but his estate enabled Amanda to do what she wanted and start a business of her own.

She had kept her gallery job very reasonably for three years after her father died, and had bought the handsome apartment she still lived in. And at twenty-five, she started her gallery, and was joined a year later by Pascal Leblanc.

She had realized by then that she needed a partner to help her run the business, and he was the perfect one. Talented, conscientious, and reliable, he had more experience in the art world than she did, and they got along well. At thirty-nine, she had been without a family for seventeen years now, and was a highly responsible woman, with a good head on her shoulders. She missed having a mother and father, or any relatives, but she had adjusted to it, and Pascal had several times invited her to spend holidays with him and his parents. In recent years, she had gone skiing with friends at Christmas, and paid as little attention as possible to the holiday. It was easier for her that way and made her feel less like an orphan.

There was nothing pathetic about her. She was a beautiful, successful woman with a career and a business she loved, and artists whom she represented and treated like her own children. She had an active social life, a home she loved, and a toy poodle named Lulu she said was her soulmate. She took Lulu everywhere with her. She was a small white ball of fluff, who was fierce when she defended her mistress, and very possessive of her.

Amanda never really thought about having children or a husband. She felt that it would happen someday if it was meant to, and in the meantime, she was enjoying her life to the fullest. She didn't feel as though she was missing anything she desperately needed. She was startled to realize that she was turning forty. It seemed like a major milestone to her, and she couldn't believe it had come so fast. It seemed like only yesterday when she had graduated from college in New York, and then, so few months later, she had found herself entirely on her own. That had been a hard time for her. But her life now was easy in comparison, and in perfect order. She'd had a series of predictable relationships in her twenties, a penchant for sexy bad boys, which had cured her of men like them forever. They no longer held any allure for her by the time she was thirty. Pascal had always sounded the alarm bells when he spotted a particularly bad one, and there had been several. Amanda had always managed to extricate herself with grace, and was wise about it.

Her inheritance, no matter how discreet she was, had attracted a number of fortune hunters. Most of them were obvious enough for her to see them clearly. She had been taken in once or twice, but not for long. At thirty-three she'd had a painful affair with a married man, her first and only relationship of its kind. He had insisted that he and his wife were "almost" divorced, and had an "understanding," although they still lived in the same apartment, for "the children's sake" and for financial reasons. He wasn't eager to lose half of everything he had in a divorce. The affair had gone on for three years, despite Pascal's warnings. Amanda's married lover had never left his wife, as their alleged understanding was apparently unilateral. His wife had hired a private detective, who had taken photographs of Amanda with her married lover. His wife had threatened to take everything he had, not just half, and Amanda had finally left him with a broken heart and shattered illusions.

It had been three years since it ended, and she hadn't had another deeply serious relationship since, and didn't really want one. She wasn't bitter, she was cautious, and she no longer fully trusted her own judgment. She'd gone out with several other men but hadn't fallen in love again. She enjoyed the fact that her life was pain-free now. She wasn't suffering, sad, or disappointed. She liked having an orderly life, and a man she could count on. There were no candidates offering her that at the moment, and she didn't really care.

In sharp contrast, Pascal had been in love eight or ten times during Amanda's three-year hiatus from serious romance. She said she loved how easy her life was now, and Pascal believed her, and envied her light, untroubled heart and calm demeanor. He was always in the throes of some unbridled agony involving a woman who either didn't love him enough, was stalking him, or had another lover and was cheating on him. Amanda knew all the standard scenarios by heart. But he was a great and reliable business partner and a good friend, though he seemed to have a need for chaos in his personal life. She forgave him, as long as his distractions didn't hurt the business. She was very clear about that, and so was he.

She didn't even know what sort of man she'd want now, but definitely not a married one. She had a dream about having an equal relationship of some kind with a man, but so far it had never happened. There was always some form of glaring inequity that kept her from any desire to make the alliance permanent. She was much too comfortable as she was to let any man ruin it for her, no matter how attractive he was. No one seemed worth that to her. Pascal was sorry for her on that score, but no other. He admired her unfailing ability to keep her life in good order. She'd been doing it for a long time, and her father had prepared her well. He left her the means to be secure forever, if she kept what she had and invested wisely. She was always sensible about money.

Pascal's parents were comfortable, with the remains of dwindling family fortunes, but they weren't wealthy. They were the fairly typical descendants of people of a respectable bloodline, and he worked hard to compensate for what he didn't have and wouldn't inherit. He had no illusions about it and was a hard worker. He and Amanda both were. Amanda worked harder than anyone he knew. He respected her a good deal for it, since she didn't have to. She was set for life, especially now with a successful gallery. Her business had grown exponentially since she started it. They did well and had several important clients. Pascal's main contributions had been his training and talent, a little money he had saved, and several solid gallery and museum jobs to his credit. Amanda had had only dreams and talent when she started, and her inheritance, and now she had fourteen years of experience and the self-confidence that came with it.

She sat on the terrace of her apartment, drinking her morning coffee and enjoying the view of the Eiffel Tower, as she did every day. Lulu was sitting politely at her feet, waiting for her ritual piece of toast, which Amanda handed her in small bites.

The weather was beginning to turn warm in the early days of spring. Amanda loved Paris at any time of year, even when the weather was gray and dark, which made the first of the spring weather even more enjoyable. She couldn't imagine living anywhere else now. Her six years in the States, between twelve and fourteen and then for college, seemed like a distant dream now, part of another life. She went to New York on business from time to time, which reminded her of her mother and made her nostalgic, but it seemed foreign to her. Paris was part of her soul, New York her history.

She had made friends in college but had lost touch with most of them over the years once she went back to France. One or two of them would look her up occasionally when they came to Paris, and she would have lunch with them. All of her college friends were married now and had children of nearly college age themselves. Amanda couldn't imagine what that must be like.

Many of her French friends were married too, but most of them married later, or had children and didn't marry at all, particularly among her artists, who were indifferent to what they considered old-fashioned traditions, which they thought were meaningless in today's world. Personally, Amanda didn't think that marriage was "necessary," but she thought it must be more reassuring to children if their parents were married. Whenever she said something like that, Pascal accused her of being American, since he assumed that Americans were more puritanical than the French. He wasn't entirely wrong.

It was a pet peeve of Amanda's that when she said anything men didn't agree with they called her American. She had certain standards, some of them old-fashioned, which she believed in. Like being faithful to one's spouse, which wasn't always the case in France. She had had ample opportunity to see how her father's infidelities had damaged and finally destroyed her parents' marriage and broken her mother's heart, and she had had a taste of that herself with her one married lover. Someone always got hurt if one spouse cheated on the other.

Even though it had been legal in France now for many years, most Frenchmen shied away from divorce and the financial impact of it. They preferred to stay with a spouse they no longer loved, and work around it.

Having a mistress was still a common occurrence in France, and Amanda had a particular aversion to it, although she knew that many of her friends weren't faithful to their spouses. She'd had the same argument with the married men who asked her out. They all insisted that they had an arrangement with their wives, which rarely was as neat and tidy and simple as they claimed. Pascal accused her of being American on that subject too.

"It's not about being 'American,'" she always insisted. "It's about being decent and honest. If you date married men, someone always gets hurt."

"Love is dangerous, that's half the fun," Pascal said, and she knew he had had affairs with several married women. But he hadn't been in love with them, so he didn't get hurt. It was just for fun. "Besides, you're missing opportunities. At our age, everyone we know is married. You might meet someone you really love, and he can always get divorced later."

"Which makes me the bitch who broke up his marriage, so his

children hate me. And most of those guys don't leave their wives. I don't like complications, or getting tangled up in a mess."

"That's what I mean," he had often said smugly, "you're American. Americans get divorced, and then they fall in love with someone else, most of the time anyway."

"Fine. Then I'm American," Amanda said, exasperated. "But that makes much more sense to me."

"Why should they get divorced if they have no one else to go to? Why disrupt everyone for nothing? And spend all that money on a divorce?"

"Because it's cleaner. My mother never forgave my father for the times he cheated on her, and he wasn't looking for another woman, he was just having fun. He told me that himself when I was in college. She never forgave him, and he always regretted it. He said he never met another woman as wonderful as she was. She was pretty terrific. And I don't think she was ever unfaithful to him."

"I don't think my parents have ever been unfaithful either," Pascal admitted to her. "But they lead a very small life." His father was a retired banker, and his mother had never worked. They lived in Normandy now, in a cozy, pretty house, an eighteenth-century cottage. "I can't imagine being faithful to anyone," Pascal had admitted to her for years. "I would die of boredom."

"I wouldn't marry you either," Amanda said firmly, laughing. The idea had never appealed to either of them. Their philosophies about love and marriage were at opposite extremes.

"I don't understand you. You're the most independent woman I know, and you have absolutely antiquated ideas about relationships."

"That's probably why I haven't had a serious date in three years. I only go out with single men, and at my age there are none left, except the weirdos no one wants." But she wasn't unhappy with her lot in life, which he knew too. She seemed perfectly content, while he was always looking for someone better than he already had. He'd been that way for all of his dating life. He loved his parents, but he didn't want to end up like them, with a dreary, unexciting life. Spending a weekend with them made him nervous, as though their lifestyle was contagious, or some sort of family curse. He hated the thought of being with the same person forever. Amanda was somewhat leery of that concept too, which was why she was happy as she was, and she didn't want to make a mistake. Her worst nightmare was another married man like the one she'd had. She was careful not to fall into that trap again.

But other than their ideas about romance, she and Pascal got on extremely well, and he was a hard worker, as she was.

Amanda left the terrace, put her cup and plate in the sink for the daily housekeeper to find later, and went to dress for work, while Lulu followed her to the bathroom and waited patiently while she showered and dressed.

She wore black jeans to work, a big soft pink sweater, a black peacoat, and black cowboy boots she'd had since college and loved. She carried Lulu in a Birkin and walked to work. She went straight to her office to check her emails, while the tiny white poodle climbed into her pink bed next to Amanda's desk, curled up, and went to sleep, and Amanda continued reading, after hanging up her jacket. Her office was big and bright and cheerful with some of her favorite paintings on the walls, including a big Damien Hirst across from her desk, and an easel to show clients paintings in her private office.

Her assistant, Margo, brought her a cup of coffee and set it down next to her, while Amanda smiled, waved, and continued reading, and frowned when she read the last email, just as Pascal walked into her office. They looked like brother and sister. He was tall, but just as blond as she was, with deep blue eyes, and he sprawled out in the chair across from her desk. His hair was tousled, which gave him a boyish look, and he looked a dozen years younger than forty-four. He was wearing jeans with a well-cut tweed jacket, a pale blue Hermès shirt, and brown suede shoes. He had a sexy casual look, and women of all ages melted when they saw him, which Amanda thought was amusing and teased him about.

"That's not a happy face," Pascal said, smiling at her. "Is someone returning an expensive painting?"

"Worse than that." Amanda looked at him. He had become the closest thing she had to family in the years they had been working together. He was the brother she'd never had. "The de Beaumonts are giving one of their impromptu dinner parties."

He frowned in response. "Oh, that is bad news. For you." He grinned. "As I recall, it's your turn. I went to the last one. Inedible food, deadly guests, and accordion music. Put your party shoes on." The de Beaumonts were among their best customers and had an important art collection they added to constantly. They also gave the worst dinner parties in Paris, usually on the spur of the moment, but considered them command performances despite the short notice, and expected everyone to come. And because they were rich and important, most of the people they invited accepted. They were nice people, but served terrible food, and the accordion music was the icing on the cake. Mr. de Beaumont joined the accordionist with an accordion of his own after dinner, if he had too much to drink, which he usually did.

"I can't. The dinner party is tonight. I'm probably an add-on anyway, to even out their numbers if they need a single woman. Someone must have canceled. I'm taking Peggy and Brad Abloff to dinner," she said. They were a young American couple, talented artists, and fun to be with. The gallery had been representing them for the last year, with great results. "I don't want to disappoint them and cancel at the last minute."

"You have to," Pascal said without hesitating, and stood up. "You can't turn the de Beaumonts down. Even if you're an add-on, they'll be insulted if you don't go."

"If you go tonight, I'll go to the next two," Amanda bargained with him in a pleading tone, and he shook his head and stood up with a boyish grin.

"No way. That's worth at least four dinners. I have a hot date with a lingerie model tonight. I've been trying to get her to go out with me for a month, and she just broke up with her boyfriend. I'm taking her out to console her."

"Poor girl. Talk about a wolf in wolf's clothing."

"Her boyfriend was a jerk. I'm a vast improvement. And I'm taking her to the Voltaire," one of the best and fanciest small restaurants in Paris. Pascal was generous with his dates.

"She's a lucky girl," Amanda said with a sigh. "And I'm screwed. What'll I tell Peggy and Brad?"

"That you're going to have dinner with the people who are going to buy their next pieces. Give them another night, they won't mind." Amanda was more motherly with their artists. Pascal had less patience with them.

"No, but I do. I nearly fell asleep at the last one, and Francois de Beaumont played the accordion until one A.M.," Amanda said, mournfully.

"It's for a good cause," Pascal assured her as he left her office, excited about his own plans for that night. The lingerie model was the prettiest woman he had met in years. He loved the beginning of a romance more than anything in the world.

Amanda emailed Virginie de Beaumont and accepted "with pleasure" despite the last-minute invitation, which botched up her plans for an evening she had been looking forward to. And then she wrote to the two young artists, apologized profusely, and asked them to suggest another night, which they did five minutes later, for a night Amanda was free anyway. But she dreaded another painfully boring evening at the de Beaumonts', with their equally tedious friends. It was one of the few things she disliked about her job, but they were sweet people. They just served bad food and had boring friends, and Amanda hated accordion music. But as Pascal said, it was all for a good cause. The success of the gallery was based on the high quality of the work she and Pascal sold, their skill in finding new artists, and their warm relations with their clients. And if she had to listen to accordion music in the process, so be it. It was a small price to pay for the success they enjoyed.

The rest of the day she reviewed slides of new artists' work. She often found new undiscovered talent in those slides and went over them carefully. At six o'clock she went home to dress for dinner, and Pascal sent her a text.

"Have a great time tonight!" he gloated, and she shot back an answer.

"I hate you! I hope your hot date is more boring than the de Beaumonts."

"Not humanly possible," he responded, with an emoji of a man falling out of his chair, laughing, and she went to pick out something to wear and hoped she didn't fall asleep at dinner. She almost had the last time she went.

Lulu gave her a dirty look and climbed into her bed, when she saw that Amanda had put her coat on and was going out without her. And all Amanda wished was that she was staying home with her, or going to dinner with the two young artists at one of their favorite bistros. She softly closed the door behind her and headed out for an evening of the dreaded accordion music, trying to think of something suitably rude to text to Pascal.

Chapter 2

Amanda wore a simple black cocktail dress that was only slightly sexy to dinner. It was short, but still respectable. Her long blond hair was in a bun. The de Beaumonts were very proper, and seemed more traditional than the somewhat daring art they bought. Their home was very expensively decorated by one of the best decorators in Paris, and they owned a chateau two hours out of the city, where many of their larger pieces were. The Paris home was smaller than the chateau but still very spacious, with a spectacular garden that was lit and that one could see from the dining room. All the flowers in it were white, and had just begun to bloom. The de Beaumonts had fourteen for dinner, which made Amanda realize that she had been invited so there wouldn't be thirteen guests. One of the guests mentioned that his wife had a bad cold and had canceled, so, as Amanda had suspected, they had invited her. Most of the guests were in their sixties and seventies, and Amanda was the youngest person there. The de Beaumonts had their decorator to dinner too, a well-known older man who had done some of the finest homes in Paris. He and Amanda had met several times, and they chatted before dinner, while Virginie de Beaumont fluttered around among her guests and Francois de Beaumont talked business with some of the men. He had invested family money in two television stations, and multiplied their fortune unimaginably. Virginie wore only haute couture clothes, and had a huge diamond on her left hand. They had unlimited money, but less taste, except for the art pieces they bought. They were kind, well-meaning people, and had three sons Amanda's age who were married and had several children each. Amanda had met the sons, but they didn't share their parents' interest in contemporary art and had never bought anything from her.

After chatting with the decorator, Amanda spoke with two of the guests' wives, who were talking about their summer plans. Several of them had chateaux, and their grandchildren were coming to stay with them after school let out. The conversation was pretty much what it always was at the de Beaumont dinners, very domestic among the women, and business among the men. They sat down promptly at eight o'clock, which was early for Paris, and only half an hour after they arrived.

As they arrived at the table laden with flowers in the dining room, Amanda saw that she was sitting next to one of the older men, who greeted her pleasantly, and then turned to the woman on his other side, whom he knew. Amanda noticed that she had an empty seat next to her just as she heard the doorbell ring, and a man in a dark suit rushed into the dining room with apologies to their hostess, who kissed him on both cheeks and pointed to the only empty seat. He came quickly to sit next to Amanda and smiled at her as he slipped into his chair. She couldn't help noticing that he was strikingly handsome and looked very distinguished in a suit, white shirt, and navy Hermès tie, he had impeccably cut brown hair, almost black, with gray at the temples. He looked to be somewhere in his mid- to late forties and introduced himself with a pleasant smile.

"Sorry for the late arrival," he said, with a smile that lit up his face. He had warm brown eyes and chiseled features, looked very athletic with broad shoulders, and had good manners as he spoke to her. "I got caught in a meeting. I don't usually get out of the office this early. I don't suppose Francois stays late at the office much anymore." Francois de Beaumont wasn't retired yet, but he was getting there. Her seatmate paid close attention to Amanda as he spoke to her, and she had the feeling he was looking her over, and wondering who she was. Neither of them looked as though they belonged there with a much older group of guests. The man on Amanda's left looked vital and alive, and there was a powerful electricity about him that was easy to respond to. He had introduced himself as Olivier Saint Albin. The name was familiar, but Amanda couldn't place it and it didn't ring any immediate bells. "How do you know the de Beaumonts?" he asked her directly.

"They buy art from me. I own a gallery," she said simply, and he nodded, and seemed interested. Amanda felt stupid doing so, but almost by reflex glanced at his left hand to see if he was wearing a ring, as he ate the somewhat unruly salad, which was their first course, with chunks of lobster in it. The food looked a little better than usual, as the waiters who served their dinner parties put the heavily laden plate in front of each of them. And she saw clearly that Olivier Saint Albin wasn't wearing a wedding ring, and only a crest ring on his right hand, as many Frenchmen did, if they had a crest, which was a sign of noble ancestry.

"That's interesting. Where is your gallery?" She told him and he looked impressed. "Is it new?"

She smiled. "No, I've been there for fourteen years, almost fifteen. Are you a fan of the art world?" She didn't know why, but he didn't look it to her. She could imagine him being more interested in business than art.

"Not really," he said honestly. "I don't know anything about contemporary art, and haven't had time to get educated about it."

"It's all about what one loves. I always think that's the best way to buy art, not simply for its value." People always wanted to know which pieces were the best investment, which Amanda felt was a sad way to buy art. If you were going to live with it, you should love it, not just buy it as an investment. Francois de Beaumont had a tendency to buy art for its value. He preferred adding important artists to their collection. Virginie and their decorator picked most of the pieces they bought from Galerie Delanoe, and Amanda usually agreed with their choices. Virginie fell in love with the pieces they bought.

As they chatted, the accordionist appeared and began playing old Edith Piaf songs, starting with "La Vie en Rose," which had been a favorite of Amanda's father, but wasn't hers. She had to force herself to keep a straight face, and Olivier grinned.

"Ms. Delanoe," he whispered conspiratorially, "do I get the impression that you're not a fan of the accordion?"

"No . . . I . . . yes, well . . ." She giggled, and smiled at him. "No, I'm not," she whispered back.

"That's a shame, particularly if our host joins him after dinner." She laughed out loud then, and his smile grew broader. "There are two instruments I hate. The accordion and the harp. The harp always makes me feel that I died and went to Heaven, and I didn't notice. You must think I'm a savage who hates art and music."

"No, I don't like either instrument. The de Beaumonts always have the accordion," she informed him.

"I know. I met them through my parents, and they've been kind enough to invite me a number of times." His expression was hard to read, and she couldn't tell if he enjoyed being there or not, and she didn't want to be rude and say that she considered their dinner parties deadly.

"What do you do?" she asked, hoping it didn't sound intrusive. Well-brought-up French people were taught early not to ask overly personal questions, like about family or business.

"I'm a publisher. I ran a big publishing house for most of my career and started a small one on my own three years ago. I'm sure you've never heard of it. It's been very exciting, but we're still small."

"That's brave of you. Publishing isn't an easy business these days."

"Neither is selling art. That makes two of us who are brave. Francois has been very encouraging. He advised me that doing something entrepreneurial might be more rewarding than going back into the corporate world. I decided he was right and took the leap. It's been an incredible amount of work, but I love it. I particularly enjoy getting to know our new unknown writers and what inspires them." Amanda nodded, wondered if he was divorced, and assumed he was. She felt a little foolish and girlish for the reaction, but she was happy he hadn't been wearing a wedding ring. She hadn't met any man she liked as much or who was as fun to talk to in ages, and it would have been discouraging if the first man she found attractive in three years was married. She'd probably never see him again, but at least if she did, he was fair game. She cringed, thinking of what Pascal would have to say about it. But sitting next to Olivier was making the evening pass more quickly, and surely more pleasantly. "I'm more of a babysitter for my young writers, and I enjoy it. Our conversations become part of their process and how they build the book," he said, as the waiters removed the lobster remains and switched to clean plates and a large serving platter with rice, green beans, and some kind of chicken casserole, which looked typical of the food at these parties. Amanda hesitated when it got to her.

Olivier leaned over and whispered to her again. "I'd go light on the chicken. The sauce looks deadly. The rice and beans are safer if you're in doubt." The food they served always tasted the same, from Virginie's recipes.

"I was thinking the same thing," she said, helping herself sparingly.

"The waiter says the chicken is spicy, some kind of Indian curry. You might want to be careful if you don't like hot food."

She had taken the tiniest piece of white meat, and the chicken didn't look fully cooked. Both the rice and the string beans were plain and had been steamed, and seemed safer.

"I think the cook is very elderly. The de Beaumonts used to give big dinner parties with caterers. But we all come here for them, not for the food," he commented.

"Or the music," she whispered, and he laughed out loud, and a minute later he turned to the woman on his left and started talking to her. He had spent a long time conversing with Amanda, which he preferred, but he was supposed to divide himself evenly between the two. Amanda spoke to the older man on her right, and they struggled for topics of interest to both of them. He very kindly discussed art with her once he knew her profession. And then the dessert came, some kind of Bavarian raspberry mousse, as Francois de Beaumont went to get his accordion and Amanda successfully managed not to groan.

"I heard that," Olivier whispered to tease her.

"No, you didn't, I didn't say anything."

"No, but your face did," he said accurately. "The last time I was here we had chocolate soufflé, which was delicious. I thought we had gotten past the mousses and gelatin desserts, but now they're back. They always make me feel like I'm in school."

"Me too. I used to shoot chocolate pudding at the ceiling and it would come down on the nuns' heads," she whispered, and he laughed again.

"You must have been a charming student," he said with a warm look. "Did you eventually get expelled?" There was something very appealing about him. They were like two irreverent students whispering at the back of the classroom. He was playful and he seemed very at ease with women.

"No, my parents moved me to a different school. The nuns and I weren't compatible."

"I had the same problem with Jesuit priests. I eventually got sent to boarding school," he said, "in Switzerland." She could guess it was one of the two or three famous ones where aristocratic boys went to school. She had been happy at home with her parents, until

New York and the divorce. Before that, she and her parents had been like the Three Musketeers.

By then, their host was playing the accordion with the hired musician, and listening to it was painful. Coffee was served in the drawing room in delicate antique cups, and the two men playing accordion followed them in. But Olivier made it all bearable. She was intrigued by him. He seemed effortlessly seductive and kept the conversation light.

"You mentioned babysitting your young writers, that's what I do with my artists. I love that part of my work. They're so innocent in a way, most of them. Some of them are outrageous and very badly behaved, but most of them are adorable."

"Do you have children?" he asked her, which was a surprisingly personal question for a first meeting in polite social circles in France. She was startled and shook her head.

"I'm not married," she answered, and then was mortified because it sounded like a come-on line, which wasn't her intention. It sounded embarrassingly obvious. And as good-looking as he was, she could easily imagine that women pursued him all the time. There was a faintly flirtatious style to his conversation, but in a polite, well-brought-up way. He wasn't vulgar or presumptuous, but he was very much a man, and seemed aware of her as a woman. In her embarrassment, she didn't feel comfortable asking him if he had children and assumed he'd volunteer it if he did. The fact that he didn't told her he didn't have children either, and she wondered if he was divorced or had never been married, but didn't ask him.

She was almost sorry when he was the first to leave after coffee in the living room, apologizing to their hostess, and explaining that he was taking the Eurostar to London early the next morning and didn't want to stay out too late. He made a point of saying goodbye to Amanda, and said he hoped to see her again sometime and that he would stop by her gallery. She wondered if he was just being polite or would really stop by. She had enjoyed talking to him, which had made the evening much more bearable than she'd expected. She didn't want to leave as soon as he did, since she had no valid excuse, and she got trapped for another hour listening to the two men play their accordions, and finally escaped just before midnight. Without Olivier to add levity to it, the evening seemed endless after he left, and she was relieved to get home, take her dress off, and climb into bed with Lulu. It had been a very long evening, and the only enjoyable part had been talking to Olivier Saint Albin. She hoped he'd come to the gallery, as he had said.

She wasn't going to mention him to Pascal the next day. There was nothing to say really, except that she had been seated next to a bright, interesting guy. Olivier Saint Albin hadn't asked Amanda for her card or her number. She had mentioned the name of the gallery, so he could find her if he really wanted to. But in fact he was just friendly and polite, and the only other guest close to her age. The others were all very old and very dull, like most of the de Beaumonts' friends. She wondered why they had invited him. Possibly only because he was younger, single, and good-looking. Handsome bachelors were always welcome guests.

"So, how bad was it?" Pascal asked her, as he slid into his favorite chair facing her.

"It was the usual, nothing special, some nasty chicken dish for the main course, and raspberry mousse for dessert."

"One accordion or two?" he asked, grinning.

"Two, of course. I left at midnight, and they were still playing."

"Why is it that you don't look as miserable as usual while you're telling me about it?" he asked suspiciously.

"Because I'm a good sport, and it's your turn next time." She laughed at him. "How was your date?" she asked.

"Promising. I'm seeing her again tomorrow night." He was off and running, and looked ecstatic. "You're not off the hook yet. There's something you're not telling mè about last night." He knew her well, and she was in a good mood.

"Don't be ridiculous. You know what their dinners are like. They start with 'La Vie en Rose' and by dessert you hope you can find an excuse to leave before you die of boredom."

"True. Who did you sit next to? Not Francois, I hope. He's agony to talk to once he's drunk. He fell asleep next to me last time."

"I sat next to someone's very old husband who was very polite, and we never really talked. And someone else they'd invited, a publisher." She was sparing with the details, so Pascal wouldn't make a big deal of it. He narrowed his eyes and looked at her.

"What are you keeping from me?"

She laughed at the question. "Nothing."

"How old was he?"

"I didn't ask him. Maybe your age, or a few years older."

His eyes grew wide at her answer. "I've never seen anyone younger at their dinner table. What was he doing there?"

"His father knows them."

"Was he good-looking?"

"I don't know . . . maybe . . . probably . . . I didn't notice."

"Amanda Delanoe, you are a liar! The only man in the room close to your age, and you didn't notice if he was good-looking? Did you drink yourself blind? Is he married? Was his wife there?"

"I don't think so. And no, in that order. He wasn't wearing a wedding ring."

"That doesn't mean anything. Did you ask him?"

"Of course not. And it does mean something if he wasn't wearing a ring. In France even separated men and widowers still wear their wedding rings, as protection."

"Yes, but some don't. He may have taken it off for the evening."

"At the de Beaumonts'? Only if he's after women in their seventies. He asked if I had children, and I said no and I'm not married, not that that means anything. But he didn't mention children of his own. Most married men mention their wife at least once, as a warning signal, and if they have kids, they say so. He didn't mention either one. I'm almost sure he's single."

"Well, good for you. Do you like him?"

"Yes, as much as you can tell at a dinner party. He came late and left early. He was going to London this morning. He has his own small publishing house."

"He sounds interesting. What's his name? Let's google him." Amanda had thought of it the night before when she got home, but she didn't want to get excited about him, since she'd probably never hear from him again. He was charming, which didn't necessarily mean he was interested in her.

"Olivier Saint Albin."

"It'll probably say if he's married," Pascal said, and brought the profile up on his phone immediately with the name of Olivier's publishing house. It was called simply Saint Albin. Pascal read it carefully, and there was no mention of a wife or children. It was all professional. He handed it to Amanda and she read it too. "And I was right, you are a liar. The guy is really good-looking," he said, looking at the photograph of Olivier. "He's forty-seven years old. He sounds perfect for you. So, when are you going to see him again?"

"Probably never. He didn't ask for my number or to see me again. We just had a nice time at dinner. He said he'd stop by the gallery sometime, but he's probably very busy, that's why he was late to dinner. And he must have a girlfriend. He's too good-looking not to."

"A girlfriend is easy to get rid of," Pascal said confidently. "A wife is more complicated, although nothing is insurmountable," Pascal added, sounding very French. "If he is married, he should have dropped a hint and told you, just to keep things aboveboard."

"I agree. I don't think he is," she laughed then. "Besides, he didn't have a tan mark from a wedding ring." She knew all the signs to look for.

"It's winter, so that doesn't count. You women sure know what to notice, don't you!" he said, amused. "I'll have to remember that if I ever get married. Don't get a suntan with your wedding ring on."

"He was definitely smart and interesting and fun to talk to. And he hates the accordion too." She smiled. Pascal always knew all her secrets, but she knew his too. They were best friends.

"I don't know why, but his name does ring a bell. I think I may have met him somewhere." He was only a few years older than Pascal, and it was entirely possible. Paris was a small town in some

Triangle

ways. And they were from similar milieus. It wasn't inconceivable that they had met. "I like the sound of him for you. Does he seem like a nice guy?"

"Yes, as far as I could tell. He's very smooth. And very well brought up. He went to boarding school in Switzerland. I didn't ask which one, but I can guess. There are only a few where guys like him go to school."

"I hope he calls you," Pascal said seriously, and so did Amanda, but she didn't want to say so. She didn't want to jinx it, get her hopes up, make too much of the chance meeting, or look foolish or pathetic if he didn't. And just as she had said to Pascal, he might have a girlfriend, and probably did. She thought that more likely than a wife, since he had dropped no hints that he was married, which was how most married men gave an early warning signal, with a mention of their wife or children. But she considered it highly unlikely that a man as attractive as Olivier would have no attachments whatsoever. He was the first man in a while who had appealed to her and caught her attention, and she liked how bright and playful he was. They had been co-conspirators for the evening, at a dull dinner party. He had spiced up the evening more than the hot curry.

"I hope you hear from him," Pascal said sincerely. "He sounds interesting, and fun for you. I'll bet he calls in the next few days. He'll want to be cool for at least a few days and then he'll reach out," he said confidently. Amanda was beautiful, and a catch herself.

But much to Pascal's surprise, he didn't call her or stop by. Not in the next few days, or the following week, or the week after. Time passed, and Pascal and the model he had gone out with that same night were deeply involved by then. Within three weeks, she was staying at his apartment. And he was raving about her to Amanda, about how beautiful she was, how sexy, how smart. Amanda had heard it all before, and she knew that in a month or two, the girl would be gone. Her name was Claire, and Pascal wanted to take her to Saint-Tropez that summer, to the house he rented every year with two other bachelors. Amanda knew the story of all Pascal's love affairs. They all followed the same pattern. He was dazzled at first, blinded by the beauty and attributes of the girl in question, all of which were physical, and roughly two months later, something would go wrong, and he would discover some significant flaw he had overlooked previously, like a drug problem, or a boyfriend she was still seeing and hadn't told him about. Or one of them would cheat on the other. And the girl's fate would be sealed after that. It would take days or weeks or months, but the die was cast then, and a month or so after his big discovery, or their cheating, she would leave or be sent away in a shower of tears. Pascal would pack up her things and send them back to her, wherever she was staying, and he would mourn her for a few days, or slightly longer, and she would fade into memory rapidly. A new girl would take her place weeks later. And it would start all over again. A new face, a new girl, a new moment, a new love affair. Amanda wished Pascal would find some-one with more substance, and truly fall in love one day. But she was no longer sure it would happen. He was too afraid to bare his soul and give his heart away, so he was content with his beauty pageant of plastic dollies. It made her sad for him sometimes, but it didn't seem to bother him as much as it did her on his behalf. He didn't seem to notice that time was slipping by, that the game changed as you got older, and that one day he would feel foolish with the kind of girls he went out with. It was like living on snacks all his life, and never a real meal to fulfill him.

But Amanda was no better in some way. She was in love with a toy poodle she had convinced herself was a person. And every few years a man she thought she loved, who always disappointed her, or fell short in some way.

Pascal had thought that the man she'd met at the de Beaumonts' dinner party sounded hopeful, and like a good match for Amanda. But he never called her, which surprised Pascal, he decided he must have had a girlfriend tucked away somewhere, or even a wife, despite her being convinced that he wasn't married. Women like Amanda didn't come along every day, and he must have seen that. Pascal had a hard time believing Olivier hadn't called her, and was sorry he hadn't.

Amanda never mentioned Olivier Saint Albin again, and Pascal stopped asking. He didn't want to make her feel bad. But Amanda seemed happy with her life. Business was good at the gallery. She had found two new artists she was excited about. And eventually the model Pascal had taken out the night Amanda met Olivier went back to her old boyfriend, and they were both single again. He met a young actress shortly afterward. She eclipsed all the women who had come before her, as always happened with him.

Olivier Saint Albin faded into the mists, and Amanda seemed to have forgotten him. She never said his name to Pascal again. Only Lulu knew the truth, that she had waited for weeks, hoping he would call, and he didn't. Her heart had ached for a while, as hope died, and she told herself it didn't matter. She had Lulu to console her. She told herself she was too old for romance now anyway. It would seem ridiculous at her age. She knew better than to fall in love with a stranger. She was almost forty, which felt like a major milestone to her. And there were countless younger women to keep handsome men in their forties entertained. Even when beautiful and success- ful, it was hard to compete at thirty-nine. She tried not to think about it, and if she was meant to fall in love again, one day she would. She was happy in her life, but she thought of him from time to time. It wasn't an easy face to forget.

Chapter 3

Two months after the de Beaumonts' dinner party, Amanda went to the opening of a big Picasso show. Pascal was supposed to go with her, but he got sick two days before, and felt rotten with a fever and the flu. He didn't want to get Amanda sick too, and he felt too ill to go out.

"I'm sorry to let you down," he apologized the day of the show. "I feel awful."

"Don't worry about it. I'll be fine alone. I don't mind." She had bought a new dress for the occasion, a slinky red cocktail dress by Dior with a matching coat lined in shocking pink silk, and wore high-heeled red satin sandals. She looked in the mirror once she was dressed, with her hair wound up in a loose bun, and was pleased with the effect. She had hired a car and driver. She didn't want to have to call a cab or wait for an Uber to come home. She arrived at the Petit Palais an hour after the event began. The crowd of well-dressed important people from the art world, socialites, and celebrities was huge, and many people knew her. The Delanoe Gallery was well known and respected. She walked up the steps in her high heels, showed her invitation and ID, slipped into the crowd, and accepted a glass of champagne from a waiter passing by with a silver tray. The show had been beautifully curated as a retrospective of Picasso's work, some of which had never been publicly shown before. She was admiring a large painting, stepped backward to get a broader perspective, and bumped into someone behind her, who instinctively put his arms around her to keep her from stumbling. She turned and looked up to see who it was, and her breath caught when she saw Olivier Saint Albin. He looked as startled to see her as she was, and his face broke into a smile.

"Hello, Amanda. I've thought about you so many times. I meant to call you, but time got away from me. I've been busy with my flock of writers. You probably have too, with your artists." Amanda nodded, trying to regain her composure. She was taken by surprise to see him again. She covered her discomfiture with a smile that was convincing only because he didn't know her well. Pascal would have seen immediately how uncomfortable she was, and how ambiguous about seeing Olivier again. She'd been excited about meeting him and disappointed when he didn't call. "Have you been well?" he asked her.

"Very much so." Her smile was more genuine as she regained her balance and sense of poise. "What brings you here?" she asked, but half of Paris was there, and most of them knew her, and had stopped to say hello. The crowd swirled around them, as she handed her half-empty glass of champagne to a waiter. She had managed not to get any on her dress when she backed into Olivier. She had been graceful in his arms, and light as a feather. He had felt the warmth of her body against his, and it was a very appealing sensation. He had almost forgotten how beautiful she was, but it came back to him now in a rush. "Are you enjoying the show?" she asked him.

"I am," he said, unable to tear his gaze away from hers. She was fine now, back in control and over the surprise of seeing him again.

"Most of these paintings are privately owned and have never been shown publicly before. It's an amazing treat to see them now, all in one place. I was so in awe of that one that I stumbled back into you," she said, smiling.

"Running into you has been the best part of the evening so far," he said smoothly, subtly flirtatious with her again, but she wasn't going to fall for it this time. He had bowled her over the first time, but her guard was up now, since he'd never followed up on their first meeting, and she'd hoped he would. She felt foolish for it now. He was even better-looking than she remembered. "Can I walk around the exhibition with you? You can educate me about what I'm seeing and what period it's from. Or are you with someone?" Olivier looked suddenly awkward when he asked. It had only just occurred to him that Amanda might have a date.

"No, my partner got sick, and I came alone. I actually prefer it. It's given me a chance to really look at the art. But I'd be happy to walk around with you. I've read about the work, but I haven't seen all of it myself. I want to come back when it's not so crowded so I can take my time looking. But we can take a quick tour now."

It turned out to be a longer tour than they planned. Amanda got stopped every few feet by some collector, artist, or gallerist who wanted to talk to her. She introduced Olivier to them, and he was fascinated by her explanations to him about the paintings, and learned a lot from her in a brief time. He was normally more engaged in literature than art, and he was impressed by how knowledgeable she was. And she looked spectacular in her red dress.

"You really know your stuff," he said, admiring her. He wasn't sure what part of her mesmerized him the most, her face, her body, or her mind. She had the deepest eyes he had ever looked into, with a wealth of wisdom there.

"Picasso has always been my favorite artist." Amanda didn't tell Olivier that she had a Picasso at her apartment that she'd inherited from her father. It seemed unlikely now that Olivier would ever see it, and she didn't like to brag. He was just as subtly seductive as he had been the first time she met him, but she realized now that it wasn't personal and meant for her, it was just his style. He liked women and every encounter was a conquest. She didn't want to be one of them. His not calling had surprised and disappointed her. She didn't want to be surprised again, and was sure she would be disappointed if she let her guard down. Her aloofness made her even more alluring to him as they came back to a central point in the exhibit and she looked at him with a quizzical expression. He could sense that she didn't trust him, and she wasn't as warm and open as she had been at the dinner where they'd met. "Have you heard any good accordion music lately?" she asked him, sipping another glass of champagne, and he laughed.

"I've tried hard not to," he quipped back, "and succeeded. Have you been back to the de Beaumonts'?"

"No, but I sold them two very nice paintings the week after the dinner. So I guess it was worth it." She didn't tell him that for a while she had thought that it was worth it to meet him. But she no longer felt that way about him now anyway. She was leery of him. Without meaning to, he had hurt her. Maybe without even knowing it. She had been shocked to discover how vulnerable she still was to the charms of a man to whom she was just a chance encounter at a dinner party, a woman to talk to for a few hours and never see again. She had obviously made far less of an impression on him than he had on her. But now Olivier was just another face in the crowd, a handsome face, but not one she would ever see again after tonight. The tables had turned in the last two months, once she got over meeting him. He was a master at the art of flirtation, something she had never been good at. Real emotions were what meant everything to her.

But he managed to startle her anyway, when she finished her champagne, and gave the empty glass back to a waiter. "Do you want to have dinner with me tonight?" he asked her. She had seen everyone she had wanted to see, and toured the collection twice, once before she saw him and the second time with him.

"I . . . I should probably get home," she said vaguely. She didn't want to be exposed to his charm again. She had enough grace to get her through the cocktail hour, but an entire meal would be hard. She might let her guard down again, and was afraid she would. He was hard to resist. His smile was dazzling and took her breath away, and he seemed so pleased to see her, she almost believed it was real, but not quite. He had looked that way the first night too, and it had come to nothing, and she was sure the same would happen again. He was a practiced charmer of women. And she didn't want to be one of them.

"You might as well eat dinner, and you look too beautiful to go straight home," he said, trying to convince her. His eyes were pleading with her, which made him seem younger than he was and even more appealing. He wasn't easy to resist. "We can go somewhere simple if you don't want a big fancy meal. Whatever you like. I'm not ready to say goodbye yet." She could see it was the truth, and it touched her, in spite of her reservations about what kind of man he was. She had come to the conclusion that he was a chaser, a seducer, and a flirt, who practiced his skills effortlessly on women, and she had just been the flavor of the night at a boring dinner. She even wondered if the story about his going to London the next day was true. He might have had another date after the de Beaumont dinner, since it was early, and he had been in such a rush to leave. He might even have a girlfriend, and probably did. She didn't trust him, and wasn't sure why she had before. He had seemed so sincere when they talked that night, and then he never called.

"I suppose dinner would be all right," Amanda said with a sigh and a look of hesitation. They left the show together and took his car and driver, dismissing hers. Olivier slid in next to her, looking like he'd won the lottery, and she was cool with him, but she warmed up as they talked in the car.

He took her to a small fashionable bistro she'd been to often and liked. He was pleased to know that she came there frequently, and that it was a favorite of hers. They ordered dinner, and the conversation took off like lightning, about her gallery, his publishing house, her deep relationship with her father, her internal division between France and the U.S., his childhood, hers, first in Paris, then two years in New York, and then back to Paris again. He was fascinated by what a mixture she was between French and American. She appeared to be pure French in her appearance, style, and attitudes, and yet there was an underlying thread of something else within her which he recognized as American and found refreshing. There was an innocence to her he liked, a strength and courage, a candor about what she felt and believed that was less typical of Frenchwomen. She was very direct and straightforward, but gentle in the way she expressed herself.

"What do you feel? Do you feel more attached to either country?" he asked her, curious about her and hungry to know more.

"I'm definitely French. I was born here, I grew up here, I've spent most of my life here, but there's some American in the mix somewhere. I'm a Frenchwoman to my core, but now and then I think the Americans get it right. It's confusing at times, or maybe it adds something to who I am, and how I think."

"It seems like a nice problem to have."

"Not always," she admitted. "Sometimes the two parts of me are in conflict, and it tears me apart."

"You seem pretty whole to me." Olivier could tell that Amanda was a strong woman with definite ideas and principles. He liked that about her. She wasn't forceful about it, but he sensed that her emotions and values ran deep. Her style was European, but there was something American in there too. There was nothing oblique about her. Frenchwomen felt they had to be at times, to get what they wanted. She was very direct. You could tell where you stood with a woman like her. There was nothing hidden about her, or disguised. She put her cards on the table and wasn't afraid to be who she really was. It was incredibly appealing, a little scary at the same time, and new to him. Some Frenchwomen took pride in hiding the depths of their emotions. Amanda wasn't capable of hiding, and didn't want to. He could see in her eyes that she laid her heart bare and was willing to accept the consequences of speaking her truth. He was more and more aware of it as they spoke.

Olivier's driver took them back to her apartment after dinner, and he dropped her off. Amanda lived in a beautiful two-hundred-year-old building, and Olivier suspected her apartment was as stylish as she was. It was one of the best evenings he had spent in a long time with any woman, and he was hungry to see her again. He was glad he had run into her at the art opening and wished he had called her after the first time they'd met. He wasn't sure why he hadn't. Strong women frightened him sometimes, but Amanda wasn't aggressive about it. She was solid and stable, and her feet were firmly planted on the ground. She was the kind of woman who would give a man strength, not attempt to reduce him so she could take advantage of him. She wasn't competitive with him, she was real. Olivier could sense that she'd been hurt, and he didn't want to be the one to hurt her again. She didn't need him, but he wanted to take care of her and protect her anyway. He liked the fact that she wasn't desperate for a man and didn't seem to care that she wasn't married at nearly forty. It didn't appear to matter to her at all. She was a magnificent bird who had lived her entire lifetime without a cage and didn't want to start now, just so she could have a man.

Olivier had asked Amanda for her number on the drive back to her apartment, and this time she had a feeling that he'd call. She thanked him when he dropped her off, and didn't invite him upstairs. She walked up the stairs to her apartment slowly, thinking about him. It had been a good night for her too, and had come as a complete surprise.

The next day, Amanda got to her office early and was at her computer when Pascal came to the gallery, looking like death, but he said he no longer had a fever and had to catch up on work.

"How was the Picasso show?" he asked her, wearing an old sweater with holes in it that he always wore when he was sick or depressed, with torn jeans and beat-up sneakers.

"Terrific," she said, glancing up from her computer. She knew what it meant when he wore his holey sweater. "You look like you should still be in bed."

"I'm okay. I'm sorry I didn't go with you last night," he apologized again.

"They wouldn't have let you in, in that sweater." She laughed at him. "Do you want a cup of tea?"

"No, thanks." They were still talking when the delivery truck from a very fancy florist arrived, and three dozen tall blood-red roses in a vase were delivered to her desk. She was so startled she didn't guess who they were from at first. Pascal stared at them, and then at Amanda.

"Just how spectacular was the show and whom did you do what to, to get roses like that?" She laughed at the look on his face and read the card. It said, "Thank you for a magnificent evening. Lunch today? I'm already having withdrawals after last night. Olivier."

"What are there, a hundred roses in that vase?" Pascal asked her. She counted in answer to the question.

"Three dozen," she said innocently. "And I actually didn't do any-thing. All I did was eat dinner."

"With whom? The president of France?" She laughed.

"I ran into Olivier Saint Albin. Literally. I stepped backward and nearly fell over him."

"Did you ask him the question? Is he married?"

"Of course not, it would have been awkward. Hi, I haven't heard from you in two months, and by the way, are you married? And be-sides it's redundant. I'm sure he isn't. I don't need to ask him. He acts single," she said with certainty. The question hadn't even crossed her mind all night.

"I don't think single men send flowers like that," Pascal said, look-ing worried. "Only guilty married ones do."

"I don't think so. My married mistake took me to every rotten In-dian restaurant in the suburbs outside Paris and was afraid to be seen on the street with me. I had food poisoning three times, the restaurants were so bad. Olivier took me to the Voltaire, in plain sight of half of Paris. He's not hiding. And besides, he wouldn't send me flowers like this if he were married. It wouldn't be appropriate," she said firmly, and Pascal rolled his eyes.

"Hello, New York," he said cynically. "That's your logical Ameri-can side talking. Your French side knows better. In France, being married would not stop him from sending you roses, or asking you out, or a lot of other things."

"He's not trying to hide me, Pascal," Amanda insisted.

"This one is braver and has more style," Pascal pointed out. "Guys like him are rarely single. They're married or have a girlfriend. You need to ask him the question, unless you don't care if he's married or attached to someone. If you care, ask, just so you know. Then you can do whatever you want, either way."

"All right, all right." Pascal was right, but Amanda didn't want to hear it, or ask Olivier the question. Pascal shuffled off to his office then, worried about her. Judging by the excess of roses, clearly Olivier was interested in her now. And men like him were hard to resist.

Olivier called her a few minutes later about lunch, and offered to pick her up at the gallery and take her to the Fontaine de Mars for lunch, another popular, fashionable restaurant on the Left Bank. She told him she preferred to meet him there. She didn't want to get Pascal more wound up than he already was, after the roses.

She arrived at the restaurant right on time, and Olivier was waiting for her at a corner table where they wouldn't be disturbed. The owner of the restaurant knew both of them and seemed surprised to see them together, but she was warm and hospitable, and sent the waiter over to take their order. The restaurant was full and they both knew people there. He was definitely not hiding her.

As soon as they ordered, they didn't stop talking for the next two hours. Olivier told Amanda about his young authors, who were the most promising and who his favorites were. He spoke of them fondly, and she shared stories and concerns about her artists, as if each of them were talking about their respective children. It was obvious how much their careers meant to both of them, and that work had replaced many things in their lives. Amanda didn't want to ask him why he had never married or had children, and felt it was too personal and too soon to ask. Her French reserve took over and she was absolutely certain he would tell her if he had a wife, or an ex-wife, and children. He would have volunteered the information. She didn't want to play detective and interrogate him, which seemed rude. It was very obvious now that he was courting her. She liked him better than any man she'd met in years. He was handsome, exciting, intelligent, creative, and fun to talk to. It was equally obvious that he was just as taken with her.

They greeted people on the way out and he introduced her to those he knew, and she did the same. They walked together for a few blocks after lunch. He wanted to have dinner with her again in the next few days. She took a cab back to the gallery when she left him. Some books he had mentioned to her arrived at the gallery by messenger that afternoon. They were by the authors he had told her about, his favorite protégés he was so proud of.

Amanda tried to remind herself how much easier her life was without a man. She hadn't put her heart on the line for the last three years, and it had gotten badly battered the last time she had. But she strongly believed that Olivier was different, and that he wouldn't hurt her. He seemed like a warm, compassionate, honest person, and she instinctively trusted him.

She could hear alarm bells going off in her head, but it was already too late. Her heart beat faster every time she thought about him. It was a heady feeling she had almost forgotten and thought would never happen again, and now it had. Between their evening the night before, the roses he had sent, and their lunch date, when the floodgates had opened even further, it was hard to stem the tides. She let the warmth of it wash over her as she tried to do some work at her desk. There was something so appealing about the beginning of a romance, and she loved his style and warmth.

Pascal came by and asked how lunch was, with an anxious look.

"It was fine," she said casually, not wanting to let him know how strong the feelings were on both sides.

"Something tells me there's a lot going on here," he said, watching her. "Don't forget this is the same guy who didn't call you for two months." He still remembered how sad she looked then, and she barely knew the man.

"I'm fine," she said, trying to reassure him, and he went back to his own office. She was faintly annoyed that he was being overprotective, and so distrustful of Olivier, to spoil her fun.

She had finally gotten some work done, managing not to think about Olivier for two hours, when her assistant told her there was a call for her. She assumed it was Olivier, took the call without asking her who it was, and heard an unfamiliar man's voice on the phone.

"Amanda?" the voice said cautiously. "It's Tom." She had no idea who it was. "Tom Quinlan." The memories came rushing back at the sound of his name. He had been her boyfriend for a year when they were both at NYU. He had been a year ahead of her, and he had transferred to Stanford. He was from San Francisco and Stanford had been his first-choice school. He had finally gotten in on the third try. He had wanted to continue their relationship bicoastally, but it had already played out for her, and she refused. He had been loving and kind and gentle most of the time, but he was also possessive and had a jealous streak. She didn't see how that could work from three thousand miles away, and they broke up when he left. She hadn't spoken to him since she was nineteen, twenty years ago. He had written to her a few times over the years, wanting to reconnect, and had finally given up. And now, here he was. She couldn't imagine why he had called her. He had been her first big romance, a decent kid and a star student. She had heard from him when he graduated from Stanford Law School magna cum laude. She was back in Paris and had just opened the gallery then. She had written to congratulate him and didn't hear from him again.

"I got to Paris yesterday, and looked you up on the internet," Tom explained. "I'm on sabbatical from the law firm I work for in L.A. I'm a partner now. I got divorced six months ago, and I've always wanted to write a book, a thriller. So I took a year off, and here I am. I thought it would be fun to get together and catch up. Are you married?" he asked.

"No, I'm not. Do you have kids?"

"We didn't want any. It's just as well, the way things worked out. My ex-wife is an attorney too. She was managing partner of her firm, she still is. She's a bankruptcy lawyer and has done well at it."

"What made you come to Paris? Do you have friends here?" It seemed so odd to be hearing from Tom now. He really was a ghost from the past.

"I don't know a soul, but I've always loved the city. It's magical, and it seems like a good place to write. I rented a small apartment. I found it online. It's the size of a matchbox, but it's big enough for me and my computer. I wanted a change of scene for a while, so I took the sabbatical."

"That's very brave of you," she said, as her college days rushed back into her memory. She had fond memories of Tom, with twenty years' distance from them.

"Can I take you to dinner?" he asked hopefully.

"Sure. Or lunch."

"Are you free tomorrow night?" He was a stranger to her now, but in her mind he was still an awkward twenty-year-old boy. They had been madly in love for a year, and then he left and they both grew up.

"Sure," she said. They had had a good time together.

"How about L'Ami Louis? I hear it's great." She smiled when he suggested it. It was the restaurant that all Americans visiting Paris loved. It wasn't one of her favorites, but it would probably be his.

"I'll meet you there," she promised, and they agreed to a time.

They hung up a minute later and she sat staring into space at her desk. Pascal had walked in and out twice while she was on the phone with Tom.

"Who was that?" he asked, curious.

"My college boyfriend when I was nineteen. I haven't spoken to him in twenty years. He's in Paris to write a book, on a year's sabbatical. He's an attorney in L.A. He just got divorced, so he came to Paris. My life is getting crazier by the day."

Pascal grinned as he looked at her. "Now you have two men chasing you," he said, amused.

"No one is chasing me. This is just the beginning with Olivier. And Tom is a childhood memory, that's all. He's an old friend. He called because I'm the only person he knows here. It sounds a little crazy for him to come here for a year, but people do crazy things. And I can spare an evening to have dinner with an old friend."

"They're still two men. One loved you twenty years ago, and the other one is falling in love with you now. Not bad for a woman who says she's happy alone." Pascal laughed as he left her office, and Amanda got ready to leave. Even she had to admit that life was strange. It would be fun seeing Tom and reminiscing over their college days. It all seemed so far away. It was half a lifetime ago. And Olivier was the man she was falling in love with now. She smiled at the vase of roses on her desk, turned off the lights, and left for the day. Pascal was just driving away as she got into her car, and he waved at her with a smile. All he wanted for her was a good man in her life, whoever that turned out to be. And her life was suddenly getting interesting, with two men who had landed in her lap at the same time.

Chapter 4

Amanda wondered if she and Tom would recognize each other. Twenty years was a long time, and she knew she had changed, and Tom probably had too. She drove to L'Ami Louis on the rue du Vertbois in the 3rd Arrondissement, parked her car, and walked to the restaurant. When any of her college friends had come to Paris long ago, it was the one place they wanted to have dinner. It was a small, crowded, noisy restaurant, best known for its chicken, and she hadn't been there since the last of her old school friends had visited, years before.

Tom was waiting for her outside the restaurant, and she smiled as she looked at him. He hadn't changed at all. He was still tall, broad-shouldered, and athletic, with dark brown hair. He was as wholesome and clean-cut as ever, like a poster for the Marines. One would have recognized him as an American anywhere. He was wearing khakis, loafers, and a blue button-down shirt, exactly as he had when they dated in college. She had been the little French girl he was in love with then. Seeing him didn't rekindle any of her old feelings for him. He still looked like a boy to her, with the same youthful grin. He gave her a crushing hug and put an arm around her as they walked into the restaurant, and she asked for the table she had reserved. He glanced around, pleased by the ambiance of the restaurant he'd suggested, and she smiled, hearing English spoken, with American accents, at every table. No one French that she knew ever went there, but Tom was happy, and delighted to see her.

He told her about his work as a lawyer In Los Angeles, and how disappointing his marriage had been. "Cynthia is a ballbuster, and a very successful lawyer. All she cares about is making money. The divorce was a relief. I'm glad we never had kids. I hope I never have to see her again." It seemed odd to Amanda not to see or speak to someone he'd been married to for fourteen years, but she knew some couples ended that way, without children. It seemed sad to her.

"Maybe you'll meet someone here," Amanda said to cheer him. He still had the intensity he'd had at nineteen, so earnest about everything, but she could see sadness in his eyes now. The only time his face lit up was when he talked about the book he was going to write. He had started it in L.A. and wanted to finish it here. Being with him reminded her of her student days in New York, when she had discovered that she didn't want to live in the States and wanted to come home to France. Talking to Tom made her realize again how French she felt, and how little she had in common with him. Their points of view were entirely different, even more so than they had been twenty years before when their romance ended.

"Do you miss New York?" he asked her over dinner.

"Never. I'm happy here. This was always home. I had to live there while I went to school to understand that. I go to New York for work a few times a year. After a few days, all I want to do is get back. It never felt like home to me, even when I was there with my mother for two years. I missed Paris."

"I'm sorry about your dad," he said respectfully. Tom had met him once when her father visited. Armand had been afraid that she would want to stay in the U.S. and marry Tom. But Tom's transferring to Stanford had put an easy end to their relationship. She had been ready to move on by then, although Tom had tried to hang on to her, but he couldn't. The distance was too great, and they were too young, their lives headed in opposite directions, even though he didn't want to see it. But finally, he did. He had written to Amanda when her father died and had sent her an announcement when he married Cynthia while he was in law school. That was the last time she had heard from him. She had written to congratulate him, and he hadn't answered. She didn't expect him to.

"Why didn't you ever marry?" he asked her when they got to the end of dinner. He was forty, a year older than she was.

"I was never with the right man," she said honestly. "And I didn't want to. I'm comfortable the way I am. It's never been a major goal for me."

"We would have been good together," he said wistfully.

"No, we wouldn't." She had always been honest with him. "Your life was meant to be in the States. You'd always have been a foreigner here. And I wanted to come home. I would have been unhappy there. This is where I belong. I think people end up where they're meant to. I can't even imagine living in the States again. I always felt like a stranger."

"You could open a gallery in L.A.," he said, as though trying to convince her, and she smiled at him.

"I'm not a little French girl anymore, Tom. I'm a grown woman. And I want to grow old here, with my own kind. I realized how different I was when I went to NYU. I went there to feel closer to my mother after she was gone. But it showed me how different we were. I was always more French than American. Some people transplant more easily than others. I don't think I would have."

"I would have moved to France for you," he said, with a look of longing.

"You'd have hated it after a few years. The French are not so easy to live with, and they're not always kind to foreigners." She had no American friends in Paris, but she didn't say that to him. She didn't want to be rude. "What's your book about?" she asked him, to change the subject, and he smiled as soon as she did.

"Lots of blood and guts, full of surprises. Your basic thriller. If it's any good, I'd like to get it made into a movie. I need to find an agent. It's hard to find a good one. And I have to finish the book first. That's why I took my sabbatical. I've been dreaming of writing this since I was in law school. I just never had the time. When Cynthia and I got divorced and I turned forty, I decided to do it. I want to follow my dreams now, before I get any older."

"I kind of feel that way now too," she admitted. "The gallery has been my dream, but I don't know how we got this old so fast. The years just flew by. I've been so busy building my business, and suddenly I wake up and I'm nearly forty. I still can't believe it."

"Yeah, me too," he said, as he signaled the waiter for the check. It had been an easy, relaxed evening for old times' sake. "Do you run your gallery alone?"

"No, I have a terrific partner. He's taught me a lot about the business."

Tom's brow furrowed as he listened. "Is he your boyfriend?"

"No, he's my best friend, which is even better. If we were romantically involved, it would have hurt the business, and we might not have stayed together. It's much simpler this way." He relaxed again when he heard her answer, and she could see that his old jealous streak was still with him, even though they had no romantic ties now. It was the one thing she hadn't liked about him, and they had argued over it frequently. She had been ready for their relationship to end when he went back to California. She was tired of his suspicions and accusations. He had accused her several times of cheating on him, and she never had. His worries had been unfounded.

She thanked him for dinner and left him outside the restaurant. "Good luck with the book!" She smiled warmly, and he hugged her.

"You haven't changed a bit, Amanda. You still look the same, and you're still the same sweet person. I shouldn't have transferred. We might be married now if I hadn't, and had a houseful of kids."

"No, we wouldn't," she said firmly. It sounded like a nightmare to her, and she chuckled. "I'm not big on kids, and have never wanted any, so far. But you're still young. You've got lots of time to meet the right person and start over again."

"I hope so, but first the book!" he said with determination.

He stood on the sidewalk watching as she drove away. She felt sorry for him. There was something sad about him. Clearly his life hadn't turned out the way he wanted, or maybe he was just at a low point right now after the divorce. She hoped that Paris would be good for him, but she wasn't sure it would be. He was so thoroughly American. Or maybe he'd get a new outlook when he finished his book. There was clearly something missing in his life, and he kept talking about his college days as the best years he'd ever had. She had had fun then, but they were by no means her best years, and they felt like someone else's life now. He was clinging to the past because he had nothing and no one to hold on to in the present.

She told Pascal about it the next day.

"I have friends like that, who're still hanging on to their student days," Pascal said, "because their adult lives never turned out the way they hoped. It always seems pathetic to me. I was happy when my student days were over and I could get on with real life."

"Me too. I wonder if his book will be any good." Tom was smart, had been a brilliant student, and had had a talent for writing even then.

"Do you think he wants to go out with you while he's here, as more than just an old friend, I mean?" Pascal asked her, curious about the ex-boyfriend who had reappeared.

"I got that impression at dinner, and I tried to deflate that balloon pretty quickly. We have nothing in common, and my life is here. He was fine when we were in college, but we're too different. We wouldn't even be friends if we met today."

"That's how I feel every time I meet up with an old girlfriend.

When it's over it's done for me." Amanda nodded agreement, especially about someone she had dated at nineteen, and she turned her mind to other things.

Olivier called and invited her to dinner the next day, and Tom called and invited her to dinner on Saturday, and she told him she was busy. She didn't want to encourage him, or mislead him. It wouldn't be fair. He was at a low point and vulnerable after his divorce obviously, and she had no romantic interest in him. He was just a souvenir of her youth. Olivier was much more interesting, and Amanda wanted to spend time with him and get to know him better.

When they had dinner again, she told Olivier about an art fair she was going to in London, and he told her excitedly that he would be there at the same time. By pure coincidence, he was going to a book fair in London.

"Let's plan to spend some time together while we're there," he said enthusiastically. And she told him about an art opening they were doing at the gallery in Paris before that. He said he'd be delighted to come. He wanted to see more of her life and how she lived it. He had asked around and had been told the gallery had a great reputation, and so did she. He was impressed by everything she was doing, and she thought his publishing house sounded fascinating. They felt like a perfect fit in so many ways. They both loved the businesses they had started and the talented people whose careers they encouraged and watched flourish. They were both mentors of talented, creative people. Amanda was sorry she hadn't met Olivier sooner. He was doing in publishing what she was doing in art.

They went for a long walk in the Bois de Boulogne on Sunday. They held hands as they walked, he stopped her under a tree and kissed her, and he held her for a long moment afterward, savoring the feeling of her next to him in his arms.

"Where have you been all my life, Amanda?" he asked wistfully, and then smiled and kissed her again. "You have so much energy, so much passion in you. You're bursting with life."

"Pascal says it's very annoying, especially when he's hungover and I won't stop talking. I always have new ideas to make the gallery more accessible and interesting, especially for young collectors." Olivier already knew that about her, just from talking to her.

They sat down on a bench after that, and he kissed her again. They watched the dogs running, the children playing, couples kissing. It was a perfect scene for a Sunday afternoon. It made her realize how much she'd been missing by being alone, and made her want to change things now and spend more time with him, although they were both busy, she with the gallery and he with publishing. It was fun educating each other about the challenges in their work lives.

He dropped by the gallery one evening before they closed. She introduced him to Pascal, and he admitted to her afterward that Olivier was very impressive.

"But you still don't know if he's married," he reminded her. Pascal was more obsessed with asking Olivier the question than she was.

"Don't be ridiculous. He takes me to all the most popular restaurants in Paris openly. He introduces me to whoever we run into. He walks in the park with me and kisses me. Do you think he'd do any of that if he were married? If I asked him that question now, it would be insulting. I'd feel stupid and sound as though I don't trust him. And I do. He would have told me by now. Stop obsessing about it."

"You'll be a lot more insulted if his wife shows up. Some couples make strange agreements. Maybe they have an open marriage, or she's away a lot."

"Or maybe she doesn't exist except in your head. There is no way he would do any of this with me if he were married. I would bet my life on it. You're being paranoid."

"Okay, if you say so. If I were in your shoes, I'd ask him, even if the question seems redundant."

"Well, I'm not going to. I trust him."

"I can see why you would. He's a cool guy. For your sake, I'd just like to be sure he's a cool *single* guy. What are you afraid of?"

"I'm not afraid. I just don't think the question is necessary or appropriate." She and Olivier hadn't slept with each other yet, but he had mentioned going away for a weekend with her. To Venice or Rome or Lake Como, somewhere romantic. It seemed like a nice beginning to her. And they were looking forward to being in London together before that, even though they'd both be working. They had a whole future to look forward to.

Amanda and Pascal worked hard on the opening of the show they were about to hang. It was an important show for a well-known artist they had recently signed to represent, and some of their bigger clients were going to be there. She reminded Olivier, and he said he wouldn't miss it.

Tom Quinlan called her two days before the show and invited her to dinner again, and she said she didn't have time. He sounded so forlorn that she invited him to the opening too, and told him there would be lots of pretty women there. He was touched to be asked and said he'd come. He had just spent a whole day at the Louvre, and another at the Pompidou Centre. He said his book was off to a slow start and he was enjoying being in Paris. He promised to see her at the show, and then she forgot about him. She had a million details to attend to for the opening.

The night of the show, she and Pascal had everything set up perfectly. Their assistants were there to greet the guests, she had hired one of the best caterers in Paris to serve champagne and hors d'oeuvres, and almost everyone they'd invited showed up. Their new artist was pleased with the turnout, and two important art critics came to review the show. The evening was a success almost as soon as they opened their doors. Tom Quinlan came too. Amanda introduced him to Pascal, and they spent a few minutes chatting, and then Pascal had to go and greet one of their clients and Tom circulated in the crowd, meeting people. He was pleasant and personable, and mingled well. Amanda had barely had time to say hello to him, but he chatted with several artists, including the one having the show. He seemed surprisingly at ease among strangers, despite his minimal French.

Olivier came late and was vastly impressed by the guest list, and the show itself. Pascal introduced him to the artist, and Amanda joined them a few minutes later. The four of them stood talking and laughing. When she noticed Tom leaving, she went to say goodbye to him and thank him for coming.

"I'm sorry I was so busy," she apologized.

"Don't be silly, I know you're working. Is that your boyfriend?" he asked, pointing to the three men she had been talking to before she came to say goodbye.

"That's my business partner and a friend, and you met the artist." She couldn't call Olivier her boyfriend yet, they had just started dating. And it was none of Tom's business. She didn't want to feed his curiosity about her personal life.

"I just wondered. I like your partner. He's a smart guy. He's lucky that he gets to work with you," he said enviously.

"I'm not sure he'd say that," she said, laughing, as she kissed Tom on the cheek and left him as he walked through the door. She went back to the others, still milling around the gallery, drinking and talking. Olivier put an arm around her and pulled her close to him, and he stayed until the end of the party. The evening had gone beautifully, and she and Pascal were both proud of the show.

It was a long evening and a resounding success. Olivier told her again how impressed he was when he left.

She and Pascal talked about it the next day when they came to work. The reviews were excellent. The artist was thrilled, and so were they.

"I like both of your men by the way," Pascal said with a smile, and she frowned at him.

"What men?"

"The charming boyish American, and handsome, dazzling Olivier. I talked to both of them. They're both good guys. You have my approval for either one, if you want it."

"I don't. Tom is ancient history and you know it. And Olivier is just beginning." She beamed when she said his name, and it was obvious who she was interested in, but they were proceeding slowly. "He's not 'my man' yet," although she liked that idea very much, more so every day. He was being very attentive and fun to be with.

"I'm not so sure Tom considers himself ancient history," Pascal said. "He talks about your time together at NYU as though it was yesterday."

"He's probably lonely here and trying to hang on to his youth. I've made it very clear to him that I'm not interested in reviving the past."

"He looks like he's still in love with you. He didn't take his eyes off you all night."

"Well, he'd better get over it. I'm not going to exhume the past with him. We were just kids. It's twenty years later and we've grown up. I won't have lunch or dinner with him again if he doesn't understand that. I think he's just lonely after the divorce."

"He's actually a nice guy. I talked to him for a while. He's very bright. But I have to admit, I can't see you with him, even at nineteen. He'll figure it out eventually. But you could have done worse. He's intelligent, successful, in great shape, and seems like a decent person. And he's crazy about you. They both are. It's nice to have choices in life," he reminded her.

"I don't want a choice. Tom is not an option. I like Olivier a lot. He's the only man I'm interested in. What about you? I saw you with that young artist we don't represent. She's very pretty."

"She wants nothing to do with me so I'm madly in love with her," Pascal said ironically, and Amanda laughed at him. She hoped Tom Quinlan wasn't going to be a problem. She didn't like awkward situations and didn't want him to become one. "Why don't you just enjoy it?" Pascal said to her. "You haven't had two guys chasing you in all the years I've known you. It's flattering. They're not about to fight a duel and bleed all over the front steps. They're both intelligent, civilized, successful men, and finally you've got two men who appreciate you. That's not all bad. Have some fun with it."

"It makes me nervous," she said, as they sat in her office. "Tom is twenty years past our expiration date. The only reason he's interested in me is because he just got divorced. He needs to meet a new woman, not hang on to an old one. And Olivier and I need time to get to know each other." But things were going beautifully between them. And now she couldn't wait for their trip to London. It would be fun to be in another city with him, and who knew what would happen while they were there. Hopefully, by the time they got back Tom would have met someone and would have a woman to spend time with. Amanda was never going to be that person in his life again, no matter how suitable Pascal thought he was. Tom's day had come and gone. She barely remembered the time they had spent together. All that she could recall now was that she was no longer in love with him when he left. And she certainly wasn't now. The man of the hour was Olivier, and Pascal had finally admitted that he no longer thought he was married and had stopped nagging her about it. Olivier would never have behaved the way he did with her if he were married, without warning her of that fact. He was an honorable man, it was written all over him. Pascal hoped that things would work out for them. It certainly looked that way for now.

Amanda could hardly wait for the trip to London. Anything could happen. Pascal was going to babysit Lulu in Paris. He loved it when he did, which only occurred when Amanda had to go to London, because of British regulations about dogs. So she left her in Paris with Pascal. The British no longer required a six-month quarantine for dogs entering the country, as they had years before. But they did require foreign dogs to take a medication for tapeworms. And her vet said that Lulu was too small to take it, so she had to leave her in Paris. Pascal was delighted to dog-sit for her. The tiny dog was a magnet for beautiful women who couldn't wait to talk to him and fuss over "his" dog. He wondered if the artist he was pursuing liked dogs. Maybe that would do the trick. And if not, there was always another woman around the next corner. He hadn't met her yet, but eventually he always did. And Lulu would assist him with the search.

Chapter 5

The art fair in London was a small, exclusive one, attended by serious collectors and some important artists. A handful of fine galleries had exhibits there. Amanda had only brought half a dozen of her gallery's high-priced paintings, and she had appointments with some of their best British clients. It was an honor to be included in the fair, which was being held at a small hall in Mayfair on Albemarle Street, tastefully decorated and the perfect setting for high-end art.

She always stayed at Claridge's, and Olivier was staying at Brooks's club as the guest of a friend. The book fair he was attending was more of a "salon" than a fair, and was attended by a less elite crowd than Amanda's clients. He had scheduled several appointments with British authors, and a few publishers he knew well. He had a number of people to see but had promised to spend time with her in the evening. He called her on her cellphone at six o'clock. She was still talking to clients in the small booth she had set up, and they were drinking champagne. She invited Olivier to join them, and he managed to get there just before seven. The art fair was open until nine, and then people went to dinner at various fancy restaurants.

Olivier enjoyed meeting the people Amanda introduced him to, and they left the fair together when the last of her clients left at eight-thirty. He had made a reservation at Harry's Bar, where he was a member, and it was one of her favorite restaurants. They served delicious Italian food and had a very elite membership. Amanda was looking forward to spending the evening with Olivier and hearing about his meetings that day. He wanted to introduce several new British authors in France and establish an exchange with the right British publishing house to translate some of his French authors. It would add a new dimension to what he could provide for his authors now. He was creative and ambitious, and excited about his work, just as she was. They were an even match, which was new for her. There had always been an imbalance in her relationships with men before. This time she loved the idea of being with someone whose energy and goals matched hers.

They had drinks at Claridge's after dinner, and Olivier made no attempt to come upstairs. He didn't want their first night together to come at the end of a long workday, when they were both tired and distracted. He said he wanted their time together to be special, and Amanda agreed. She'd been running since eight o'clock that morning, with a breakfast meeting that started her day. By the time she left him in the lobby she was exhausted, but had loved the evening. Olivier was thoughtful and kind, well-mannered and wonderful to talk to. For the first time in her life, she felt as though she was with the right man, on the same path, headed in the same direction. So far, there hadn't been a single unpleasant moment and nothing to cause her concern. She wasn't sure how well Lulu would take to him, but he said he liked dogs.

They spent five days in London over a long holiday weekend, and on their last night, Olivier wanted to spoil Amanda and took her to Murano in Mayfair for dinner. She had concluded three important deals that day, and he had found a British publisher he wanted to work with. The trip had been a success for both of them. They had much to celebrate after their first time away together, and they had been restrained. Olivier had suggested Saint-Tropez for their first romantic weekend, which sounded like fun to her, and they had agreed to wait until then. They had just finished a delicate pasta dish, with caviar first, and were drinking a very fine bottle of Chassagne-Montrachet, when he turned to her quietly, talking about their upcoming weekend in Saint-Tropez. A friend of Olivier's was lending them his house. It sounded romantic and wonderful, and like a dream come true.

"We can go to the Hotel du Cap in Cap d'Antibes, if you prefer." It was the most exclusive hotel in Europe, Amanda had stayed there several times with her father and hadn't been back since. She couldn't justify spending that kind of money on a hotel for herself. Maybe for a honeymoon or a romantic tryst. "But we'll have more privacy at my friend's house. It's fine with me either way. We don't need to hide. I haven't discussed it with you yet, Amanda. I'm married, but my wife and I have an understanding. We lead entirely separate lives." She stared at him in silence for a minute, unable to speak. She felt as though he had just shot her in the chest, more precisely her heart, and it took her breath away. For a second, she thought she was going to faint.

"You *what?*"

"We have an understanding," he repeated in a gentle voice.

"You waited until now to tell me that you're married?" He had been courting her for over a month, with roses and dinners and kisses, and a flood of texts and phone calls. Pascal was right. She felt as though Olivier had dropped a grand piano on her chest. She could barely breathe.

"I wanted to tell you before we go away together. It doesn't change anything between us or what we've been doing until now. I'm completely free to lead my own life. But I thought you should know."

"Why didn't you tell me in the beginning?" she asked him, looking deep into his eyes, searching for the answer to her question. Was he a practiced liar, and a habitual cheater? She could find no acceptable reason why he hadn't told her.

"I wanted you to get to know me better before I told you. I wanted you to see how free I am. Stephanie, my wife, travels most of the time, and even when she's in Paris, I do what I want and so does she. There are no questions asked, no jealous scenes. The marriage was a mistake right from the beginning. We were both very young, and we didn't know each other well enough. We were from the same circles, but we're very different people. She's a very cold person, and we grew up to want very different things. She's deeply involved in equestrian circles and travels all over Europe with her horses and her friends from that world. We were strangers from the beginning, and we made the mistake of having a child to try to make the relationship work. It didn't. Children are a magnifier, and it made everything worse. Stephanie is not maternal, and she had no interest or ability to be a mother and wife."

"You have a child?" Amanda said in a choked voice. He had never mentioned that either. Everything Pascal had warned her of was true. It was her worst nightmare.

"I have two sons. They're good boys. I've been married for twenty-six years." He wanted to tell her everything now and make a clean breast of it. He thought it was time, and Amanda thought it was long overdue. "My oldest son, Guillaume, is twenty-five, and he's as horse mad as his mother. He works on a horse ranch in Argentina and plays polo. Edouard was an accident. He's twenty-three and an intern at J.P. Morgan in Geneva. They're both fine young men. I don't see a lot of them, but I was mother and father to them when they were growing up, and I spend time with them when they come home, which isn't often now. Stephanie was never able to create a warm home for them, so it was up to me. She was gone most of the time and she still is."

"Do you live in the same house when she comes home?" Amanda was getting a very different picture from the one he had presented to her for the last month, of a free man with no attachments.

"I do. She's hardly there, and we don't ask each other awkward questions."

"Why didn't you get divorced?" She was stunned by everything he had told her.

"Tradition, her family. My parents are gone now, but no one in either of our families has ever been divorced. We stayed together for the boys when they were young, and eventually you settle into a way of life, and it's easier not to take everything apart. There was no reason to. It has worked the way it's been. I could never see the point of getting divorced unless I met someone else I wanted to marry, and I never did. This seemed more respectable to us, and it makes sense financially. We're not each living on half of what I earn. Financially, supporting one household makes more sense for all of us. And she feels that being married gives her status and protection. She does what she wants and so do I. We don't interfere in each other's lives." He said it all as though it was perfectly normal and reasonable, but it wasn't to Amanda, who was shocked.

"So, you stayed married to someone you don't love?"

"I love her as a sister and a friend. She's the mother of my children." He said it with respect.

"And you date other women?"

"I have," he said, honest now, a month late from Amanda's perspective. "I haven't in a while. I've been busy working, and no one has caught my eye in a few years, until you came along, and snagged my heart." Olivier reached out to touch her hand and she pulled it away. She didn't want him to touch her now, or kiss her. He was a married man, and he had lied. Sins of omission seemed as grave to her as sins of commission. He had led her to believe he was single. And he had two sons and a wife he still lived with when she was in town. Pascal had suggested that maybe his wife was away, and he'd been right. Amanda had wanted to believe he was free, and he had wanted her to, but he was anything but. She had heard stories like this before from married men who wanted to go out with her, and even married friends. But she had no respect for the dishonest lives they were living. In her eyes, they were cheaters, all of them, no matter what kind of agreements they had.

"I must have too much American blood in my veins," she said coldly. "To me, it makes no sense to stay married to someone you don't have a real life with, and a loving relationship as a spouse. You'd have been better off divorcing and meeting someone you could share a life with." Olivier looked at her as though the concept was completely foreign to him.

"Amanda, I'm free to do as I wish. I don't lie to Stephanie. We don't discuss it. And I don't ask her what she does either. She's much more interested in her horse world than a relationship with me."

"It's a messy situation for someone else," Amanda commented. "I've only dated one married man, and it ended very badly. It turned out that his wife was a lot more interested than he thought. She had me followed by a detective, and threatened to take everything he had in a divorce. He dropped me immediately when that happened. I wasted three years of my life and wound up with what I thought was a broken heart. As it turned out, it was only bruised. It took me a year to get over it. I actually thought he was going to leave her because of me, as he always said he would."

"Then he was a liar," Olivier said quietly. "I'm not a liar, and I don't make promises I can't keep. I thought of divorcing her when I was younger, but I haven't in years. The arrangement we have works well for both of us. I am completely free emotionally, and I'm available to be with you whenever you want. I don't answer to her. It's why I didn't tell you sooner, because I wanted to explain the situation to you when I knew you better. I'm totally free, Amanda, physically and emotionally, just not legally." She wanted to believe him, but she didn't. It sounded painful and dishonest to her, and fraught with opportunities for her to get hurt. "I never spend time with her."

"Then why stay married?"

"Divorce is complicated, expensive, and embarrassing."

"So is cheating," she said bluntly.

"It's not cheating. Basically, we're separated, we just live at the same address. I don't go anywhere with her. And she doesn't expect me to, or even want me to." Amanda sighed as she listened. His explanation wasn't so different from the situation she had lived before. And she was already so taken with him. She wanted to believe him, but she didn't want to be anyone's mistress. "Do you want children?" he asked her.

"I don't know," she said. "I've never really made my mind up about it. Probably not. I'm almost forty. But it would be nice to have the option."

"That's the only case in which my situation might cause a problem. I'd have to get divorced then."

"I'm not about to get pregnant to force your hand."

"I know." Olivier could tell Amanda was an honorable person, and so was he, except for the fact that he was married, which seemed like a minor problem to him but not to her. And they hadn't even slept with each other. But she was hesitant now to get any more involved with him, or even continue to see him. She didn't want to be the other woman. It felt wrong to her. And she knew how much it hurt when it ended.

"I need to think about it," she said softly. He reminded her of how good they were together, how much they enjoyed each other, and told her he was crazy about her and in love with her. She sat in silence until he paid the check and they left the restaurant. He wanted to kiss her when he left her at her hotel in the lobby, but she wouldn't let him. She could feel herself freefalling into an abyss she didn't want to fall into. Loving a married man felt all wrong to her, and was so hard, and so painful when it went wrong. She was going to try to get over him when she got home to Paris. When he walked out of the hotel, she felt as though he had run over her heart. And this was only the beginning. She couldn't imagine living the way he described. Neither her part nor his.

When she got to her room, he sent her a text that said he loved her. But what did that mean to him? Would she live in the shadows of his life if she stayed with him? His children would hate her if they ever found out about her. He was offering her the classic role of mistress in his life. He had shown her just enough of himself to make her fall in love with him. But he hadn't shown her the whole picture or been truthful with her. What else was he hiding, and how could she respect herself as his mistress? It was the last thing she wanted. But she had fallen in love. That was the hard part, and he had concealed the most important thing about himself, that he was married. It made a huge difference, no matter what he said. And what if his wife was far more involved than he claimed? Amanda had been through it all before and had sworn she'd never do it again. She didn't answer his text.

Amanda's head was spinning when she went to bed that night, and she couldn't sleep for hours. She was too shocked to even cry. Every word he had said cut through her like a knife, and she remembered every part of his explanation as she played it over and over in her head. How could he think it would be all right with her? And how could he not have told her until now? He and his wife had stayed married for their convenience and financial comfort, so his wife could maintain her "status" as a properly married woman, and he didn't have to cut his money in half to support her. But what about Amanda's comfort? She had to be his mistress if she wanted to be with him. It was a high price for her to pay so that Olivier and Stephanie could maintain their comfort and well-being, their status quo.

She finally slept for two hours and then got up. He had sent her two more texts, assuring her that he was in love with her and had never known anyone like her. She had prided herself all her life on being a woman of integrity, and now she was supposed to sneak around with him, or openly be his mistress because everyone in the world apparently knew he was married, except her.

She still felt dazed when she paid her bill the next morning and checked out of the hotel. She took the Eurostar back to Paris, and knew that Olivier was returning to Paris that afternoon. They were supposed to have dinner that night, and now they wouldn't. She sent him a brief text canceling dinner. She needed time to digest what he had told her and get over the shock. She didn't know if she ever would. She couldn't guarantee it or even reassure him, the way she felt now. She had no idea what to do except end it. She felt as though everything between them had been canceled at dinner the night before, when he told her he was married.

* * *

She had an agonizing ride back to Paris on the train, thinking about Olivier every minute and the situation they were in. She wondered if his wife's story would be the same as his or very different. That's what had happened to her before, and she had promised herself, never again. And now here she was. It was a painful déjà vu for her. Olivier made it sound so normal. It wasn't normal for her. It was a nightmare she didn't want to live through again.

When she got to Paris, she took a cab to Pascal's apartment to pick up Lulu. She rang the bell, and he buzzed her up. She hurried up the stairs, and Lulu started barking before he even opened the door. And as soon as he did, Lulu danced in circles around Amanda, who scooped her up and held her as the little white fur ball licked her face. Amanda knew that later, after she had rejoiced at their re-union, Lulu would punish her, turn her back, and give her the cold shoulder for at least two days, as she always did after Amanda had left her with someone else, but the first minutes of seeing each other were always pure joy and celebration.

Pascal took a good look at Amanda as she walked into his apart-ment and didn't like what he saw. He knew that the trip to London had been very successful, and that they had sold all but one of the paintings they sent there, all of which were high-priced items.

"Are you okay?" he asked her. "You look pale and tired. Are you sick?"

"No, I'm fine," she said in a subdued voice that was unlike her. "I'm just tired." She seemed exhausted. She looked at Pascal then, and her eyes filled with unshed tears. "You were right," she said grimly.

"About what?" He couldn't guess what she meant.

"He's married. He told me at dinner last night. He says he waited to tell me so I could see how free he is. Supposedly, they have an 'arrangement.' How often have we heard that line of bullshit? Gregoire, the married jerk, said the same thing, only his wife didn't know about it. She thought they had a real marriage. He had never let her in on the secret of their 'arrangement.'

"Olivier claims that the marriage has been a nonevent since the beginning, and they've gone their separate ways for years. She's involved in horse shows all over the place, and travels around with her horses and horsey friends. They rarely see each other, but when she comes home, they still live together, and he thinks divorce is too expensive. So they stay married.

"What the hell is wrong with people? And how could he not tell me? He dates other women and he claims his wife doesn't care. I don't believe a word of it. Gregoire said the same thing, until his wife hired a detective and told him what a divorce was going to cost him. Olivier says his wife likes the status and protection being married to him gives her. So where does that leave me? I'm the village slut if I go out with him, and his children will hate me if they ever find out. He could at least have given me the option by telling me the truth. I swear, I didn't think he was married."

"I did, until recently," Pascal said, feeling sad for her. "You finally convinced me, and he was so open with you, more than most married men, that I finally decided it was true. Guys like him are always married. And women don't let go of husbands like that. They just make their peace with it. And he might be telling you the truth. Maybe she really doesn't care. Some women don't, as long as they get a free run with his credit cards and checkbook. And he certainly is open about you. He doesn't hide you at all." Pascal had seen it for himself.

"I don't like the fact that he lied to me," she said unhappily.

"He didn't lie to you," Pascal corrected her. "He just didn't tell you. And you didn't ask him. I wonder if he would have told you the truth if you did."

"He wanted me to see how free he is. So he's free, so what. He's still married. And I'll still be an adulterer if I go out with him. I'm not religious but I don't like it anyway. It makes me seem like a home-wrecker."

"It sounds like there's no home to wreck," Pascal said.

"What are you telling me? That you think I should just forget about his wife and go forward with him? It makes me feel dirty and dishonorable."

"I assume you've slept with him," Pascal said matter-of-factly, and she shook her head.

"No, I haven't. We were taking our time."

"Then don't, if you don't want to. You haven't done anything wrong yet."

"We were going to Saint-Tropez in a week or two. I have to end it with him. I can't go out with him in these circumstances." Olivier had called her three times while she was on the train, and she didn't return the calls when she arrived. What was there to say, except goodbye? The tears spilled onto her cheeks and she wiped them away. Pascal hugged her and felt sorry for her. "The stupid thing is that I love him. Isn't that ridiculous? I was fine without him and now it feels like a tragedy that he's married. Why are the good ones always taken?"

"Because they always are, and they never get divorced if they don't have to, for just the reasons he gave you. They think it's too much trouble and too expensive. They'd rather stay married to a woman they hate, and the wives would rather be married to cheaters than have the 'shame' of a divorce. Cheating seems a lot more shameful to me, but I've never been married or divorced, so what do I know?"

"Neither have I, and this makes it even more unappealing."

"Would you marry him if he were free?" he asked her.

"Probably. Maybe. We seemed perfect for each other."

"You still are. Except you can't marry him because he's married to someone else. There's nothing to stop you if you can live with it. He seems very committed to you."

"And he lives with his wife. The two don't compute for me." Pascal wished he could cheer her up. He could see how devastated she was, justifiably in his opinion. It was a nasty shock. Particularly since Olivier hadn't warned her. There had never been even the slightest hint that he was married. Only Pascal's suspicions, which Amanda hadn't wanted to hear.

Amanda went home a few minutes later with Lulu. Olivier didn't call her that night. She knew he'd be back in Paris by the time she went to bed, but he didn't call again. She wondered if he was with his wife, and she realized that was how it would be forever. She would always be wondering if he was with her, and if he was being truthful about how separate their lives were, or if they slept together, and even made love. She hadn't had the guts to ask him about their sleeping arrangements. Living together was bad enough, but it was what most couples who were unhappy together still did. They stayed married no matter what.

Amanda lay on her bed for hours that night, in some kind of trance, thinking and wondering what she should do. The answer seemed obvious to her. She had to stop seeing Olivier, no matter how much it hurt. She had no choice really. It reminded her of her father cheating on her mother and how much it had hurt Felicia until her dying day, and how guilty he felt about it afterward. Amanda didn't want to be part of it. She had made up her mind. It was over for her with Olivier. He had seemed so perfect for her in every way, but she couldn't do it. No matter what he said to convince her. Being Olivier's mistress was not an option she would consider, so it was ending before it had even begun. She sent him a text and told him she wouldn't see him again and he wrote back and said how sad he was, but he said he accepted her decision because he loved her. It was over. She knew she had avoided a terrible mistake, but it hurt like hell.

Chapter 6

After Amanda's last text telling Olivier she wouldn't see him, she didn't hear from him again. Day after day rolled by, and he didn't send her emails or texts. He wanted her to miss him and to give in to what he wanted. He was hoping she'd change her mind. He wanted her to be his mistress, but she was just as determined not to be. She couldn't make her peace with it. She thought about it constantly but it was against her morals and everything she believed in. She missed hearing from him and seeing him. Her life felt empty without him now. It annoyed her that she was already so hooked on him, and she hadn't even slept with him. She felt him in every fiber of her being, and his absence was a physical pain somewhere between her stomach and her heart. She tried to keep busy at work, but he crept into her thoughts, night and day.

After the first week, Tom Quinlan showed up at the gallery at lunchtime and invited Amanda to join him at a nearby restaurant. She was going to turn him down, but he looked so forlorn that she went with him in the end. She hadn't been eating lunch recently and Pascal could see that she had lost weight. She was still very pale and hadn't been wearing makeup to work. She was in mourning for Olivier, but she stuck to her guns and didn't call or text him, and he was staying away too. Their miraculous affair was over, and she just had to get used to it. There was no other way.

Amanda had a nice enough time with Tom over lunch, but it wasn't the same as Olivier. They had less to talk about with a twenty-year void behind them, and Tom had no relationship to her world, nor she to his. She was willing to be friends during his sabbatical in Paris, but she wasn't attracted to him. When he pressed her, she tried to express it as gently but clearly as she could. He interrogated her again about Olivier during lunch.

"So is the guy in the suit with the dark blue tie at the opening your boyfriend?" he asked her.

"No, he's not," she said, with an edge to her voice. "He's a friend, but I'm not seeing him right now." She didn't tell Tom it was over, to avoid giving him the impression that she was available to him.

"Why not?" Tom looked surprised.

"We have a difference of opinion about something I think is important. What about you? Have you met any nice women?"

"Not really. There's one in my building. But she doesn't speak English so all we do is smile and say 'Bonjour.'"

"Maybe that's not such a bad thing," she said. "Fewer disagreements." He laughed.

"I'm sorry you had a falling-out with your friend. He seems like a nice guy. And he's crazy about you." Tom had watched Olivier closely whenever Amanda was around. Pascal had noticed Tom watching her keenly and intensely. But Tom seemed more relaxed with her at lunch, and less intense. He gave her the impression that he had finally gotten the message that she was not going to rekindle their romance, twenty years later.

"How's the book coming?" she asked him, wanting to change the subject away from Olivier, which was a sensitive topic for her right now, even more so since she wasn't hearing from him. He had vanished as soon as they returned from London. He was gone, presumably for good, which was what she had said she wanted, but it hurt anyway. She wasn't trying to force his hand to get divorced and marry her. They didn't know each other that well. She just didn't want to be his mistress, which was the only position he had open. Amanda had too much pride and was too ethical for that. The days were long and hard, and the nights were sleepless.

Tom walked her back to the gallery after lunch. He hung around with nothing to do, and clearly wasn't working too hard on his book. He was still visiting museums and tourist attractions, which made Amanda wonder if he was serious about writing, but he said he was. She really didn't know him anymore, after twenty years.

When she got back to the gallery after lunch with Tom, Pascal was in a full-blown argument with one of their artists, an American who called himself Johnny Vegas. They had been having trouble with him for a while. He had a drinking problem, and had previously been on drugs. Pascal was sure he was using substances again, and he was two months late delivering two paintings he owed them. The artist was shouting obscenities at Pascal when Amanda arrived. She was wondering if she should call the police, but Pascal insisted he could handle it himself. Johnny Vegas took a swing at Pascal and missed him, and Pascal finally lost his temper, told him he was fired, and said they would no longer represent him. Pascal physically pushed the artist out of the gallery and locked the door.

The artist pounded on the glass door until Amanda thought he would break it, and then staggered away and disappeared around the corner.

"He needs to go back to rehab," Pascal said, smoothing his shirt down. "His girlfriend left him and he's going crazy. He's talented but we can't afford to represent him." His last gallery had fired him too. Amanda hated to see it end badly, but there was nothing else they could do.

It was a full ten days after their return from London when Olivier walked into the gallery at the end of the day, looking uncomfortable. He wasn't sure what Amanda's reaction would be, but he wanted to see her. And Pascal noticed that he looked as sick and worn out as she did. Olivier was carrying an armload of flowers, and Amanda walked right into him when she stepped out of her office.

"What are you doing here?" she said in a low voice.

"I came to see you," he said, handing her the flowers. She walked them over to her assistant, handed them to her, and asked her to find a vase. There were at least two dozen red roses mixed in with lilacs and lavender hydrangea. They were beautiful, and Margo scurried off with them to find a vase big enough to hold them.

Amanda let Olivier follow her into her office against her better judgment. Her heart had taken a leap when she first saw him, and she could still feel it pounding when they both sat down with her desk between them. She didn't want to hear anything he had to say, seeing him was hard enough. She had thought she would never see or hear from him again.

"I've been going crazy, thinking about you," he said. She looked at him and didn't respond. What could she say? He knew her position, and his situation was clear to her now and wasn't going to change.

"Why don't we see how things work out with us for a year? And if we're still in love a year from now, I'll get a divorce. That would give me time to move some money around so I don't get slaughtered. How would you feel about that?" It was a major step for him to get divorced in a year, but she doubted he'd ever do it. She assumed that his wife, his children, or his wife's family would lean on him heavily, and he would wind up telling Amanda he couldn't get divorced after all. But his offer was a major concession for him. He wanted to find a way to make it work that she'd agree to. He didn't want to lose her, and Amanda didn't want to lose herself. She had already lost him, as soon as he told her he was married.

"Can't you give us a chance, Amanda? I've never known another woman like you." She was straightforward and loving and honest and trustworthy. She was everything his wife wasn't. "I don't want to lose you. Will you at least have dinner with me so we can talk about it?" He looked desperate, and she didn't want him to leave either.

"It won't get you anywhere," she warned him, and went to get her coat and put it on. They went to L'Avenue, which was familiar and easy, and sat on the terrace, discussing the situation. They went around in circles and came out in the same place every time. By the end of dinner, they were both too tired to argue about it anymore, and he could see that he wasn't going to convince her that his being married was acceptable to her. They left the restaurant after he paid, and walked a few blocks. The evening air was warmer than it had been, and it was nice to be out with him again. She had missed him fiercely for the past ten days, ever since he had dropped the bomb of his marriage on her in London.

She started to call an Uber and he stopped her.

"I'll take you home." He had left his car with the valet and when he brought it to them, Amanda slipped in next to Olivier and looked at him. Their glamorous perfect courtship had disintegrated and had become a life-and-death battle over a crucial issue: whether or not dating a married man was okay. To her, it wasn't. But he had waited to tell her, so that she had fallen for him by the time he did. They hadn't been together for long, but long enough for her to get attached to him, and she already had dreams of the future when he told her. She didn't want to give those dreams up. But dating a married man, and being in love with him, would be an enormous challenge if she moved forward with him, and a potential heartbreak in the future for her if he never left his wife. Olivier claimed that his wife wouldn't care, but Amanda found that hard to believe. He was interesting, intelligent, successful, kind, and handsome. She couldn't imagine any woman being willing to give him up. And it all mattered to her. She also didn't want to break up a marriage, but he swore that his marriage had been dead for years. It was painful for Amanda to think of giving him up, even now. For the past month, they had seemed like a perfect match.

He drove her home, as she mulled over what they'd said during dinner, and when they got to her building, he pulled over and couldn't stop himself. He took her gently in his arms and kissed her, not sure how she'd react. But her passion was as powerful as his. He couldn't stop kissing her and she didn't want him to. They were breathless when they stopped.

"What are we going to do?" he whispered to her.

"I don't know." She didn't have the power to resist him, and no matter how free and available he said he was, he was still married, and it mattered to her. She believed in the sanctity of marriage, and she didn't want to hurt anyone else as she'd been hurt before.

They sat in the car kissing for a long time. She had missed him so acutely for the past ten days that she didn't want to leave him now. He suggested they go for a walk, just to be with her a little longer. They both got out of the car and ambled slowly down the street, his arm around her. He stopped to kiss her under a streetlamp, and she felt the magic of his touch as she stood in the circle of his arms, and when they stopped, she had an odd feeling that someone was watching them. She stiffened and he looked at her, concerned. He thought she was thinking of his being married again, but she had an odd, distracted look as she glanced over her shoulder.

"What's wrong?" he asked her gently.

"Nothing. I'm just being paranoid."

"About what?" He was instantly alert and protective.

"We had to fire one of our artists a few days ago. He's been on drugs before, and we think he is again. He's an alcoholic and he's been on and off heroin for years. He's late with everything. We've given him a million chances, but we had to sever our representation of him. He took a swing at Pascal and threatened to get even with us. I just got a weird feeling that someone was watching us. I'm sure it was my imagination and has nothing to do with him." She had a horrifying feeling then that it was Olivier's wife. Or maybe just her imagination. She already felt guilty.

"You need to be careful, Amanda," Olivier warned her, and pulled her closer to him as they walked back to her building and picked up the pace. And when they got to the front door of her building, Olivier kissed her again.

"I wasn't going to do that tonight," she said to him with a small smile. "You have a way of transporting me. I forget everything when I'm with you. All reason. The problem isn't solved, you know."

"I know it's not, but it's not insurmountable either if you give us some time. I suppose I could move out, and only stay at the house when the kids come home. They know their mother and I don't get along. They've never known it any other way. Our problems started before they were born." It still seemed to Amanda like an ugly way to live. It reminded her of her parents' fights and the unbridgeable chasm between them before they finally gave up and filed for divorce, and she and her mother had moved to New York. It was a sad time, but it was better than all the tension they had lived with before the divorce. And it was all because of her father's infidelities, which was another reason why she felt so strongly about married men having extramarital affairs. She was a staunch believer in fidelity, married or not.

Olivier waited at the door while she used the code to unlock the outer door to her building and got out her key for the apartment door upstairs.

"Can I see you tomorrow?" Olivier whispered to her, and she

wanted to resist him, but she couldn't, and as they stood there, a car suddenly pulled out of a parking space not far from where they stood and peeled away with tires squealing. She was sure the driver had been watching them, but he disappeared too quickly for her to get a good view. "Was it your drugged-out artist?" he asked her.

"I couldn't tell."

"He wouldn't come to your home, would he?"

"In theory, I think he'd more likely break a window at the gallery, but who knows what he's capable of. Someone may have given him my address without my knowing."

"I don't like this," Olivier said, frowning. "Should you hire a guard?"

"We've never had a problem before. I don't know what you do in a case like this. I think he's too mentally disordered to do any real harm, but you never know. He'll probably calm down in a few days. I think getting fired was a real shock to him. We were going to give him a show in the fall, but we couldn't anyway. He was way behind on his paintings."

"Art is a dangerous business," Olivier said, teasing her.

"So is love," Amanda whispered back. But so was life. There were risks around every corner. You never knew what could happen.

She managed to tear herself away from him and slip into the building after Olivier kissed her again. She went upstairs to her apartment where Lulu was waiting. She barked and wagged her tail at Amanda, dancing in little circles on her hind legs. She was happy Amanda was home.

She got a text from Olivier as soon as she took her coat off, and then two more. They told her how much he loved her and how grateful he was to see her and spend the evening with her. She could tell that he was treading gently with her, afraid to scare her off.

She went to brush her teeth and was putting on her nightgown when the phone rang. She was sure it was going to be Olivier again, with one last thing to tell her. She didn't look at the caller ID and smiled when she answered.

"You can't miss me already," she said when she picked it up, but there was no voice on the other end. She could hear breathing, but the caller didn't speak. He just held the phone and breathed, and the caller ID said it was a blocked number when she looked. She thought either it was the fired artist, Johnny Vegas, though he never identified himself, or it was a prank of some kind.

She had three more calls from a blocked number that night and didn't answer them. They woke her up each time. She reported it to Pascal at the gallery the next day. Amanda wanted to call the police, but Pascal pointed out that they had nothing to report since all the calls were from a blocked number. She was beginning to think it really was Johnny Vegas, who had sworn revenge on them for firing him. The breathing call had been tame, and no threats were made. So, there wasn't much to say to the police if she called them.

It was a busy week after that. She didn't see Olivier the next day, or she would have mentioned the calls. She was still trying to decide what to do about him. She felt herself sliding inexorably toward him, and wondered if she should just accept the situation as he described, and see if his wife was as unengaged as he claimed. It wasn't an ideal solution, but it was one option she had that didn't entail losing him immediately. She didn't want to give him up yet.

* * *

She was tidying some things in one of her closets on Saturday, when the doorbell rang. It took her a minute to put down some items she was holding, and when she went to the door no one was there. She looked down and saw a long white florist's box, the kind that held long-stemmed roses, and she smiled. She guessed immediately that the flowers were from Olivier. He was still courting her, hoping to overcome her concerns. She bent down to pick up the box, and it was surprisingly heavy. She juggled it awkwardly, as she stepped back into her apartment, and lost her grip on it from the excessive weight of the box. It burst open, and a long gutted fish the length of the box dropped onto her entrance floor and the carpet, its bloody entrails spilling everywhere, as a foul odor of dead fish filled the hall. She jumped back as it splashed on her, and started to cry when she saw it. She couldn't imagine who would do something like that, and she instantly thought of Johnny Vegas again. She went to her bathroom, pulled off her nightgown, covered in fish guts and blood, and stood under the shower to get the smell off her.

She called Pascal and told him what had happened. He was at the gallery. She had been planning to join him there and he told her not to come in.

"The guy's a lunatic. It's just the kind of thing he would do. I'm glad we fired him. Can you get someone to help you clean up the mess? I don't want to close the gallery to come over in case he shows up to do some mischief here."

"I can handle it," she said, revolted at the thought of the gutted fish.

The phone rang as soon as she hung up with Pascal. It was Olivier, and he could hear the panic in her voice.

"Is something wrong?"

"Yes, no . . . I . . ." She told him what had happened and burst into tears at the end of it.

"I'll be right there. I'll bring some cleaning equipment. Don't touch it. I'll deal with it when I get there." He was there in less than ten minutes, wearing rubber gardening boots, with utility gloves, some scoops, and powerful industrial chemicals to clean the carpet and the floor. She helped him as best she could, and half an hour later, they had cleaned up the mess and disposed of the fish in the rubbish bins downstairs. Amanda was still looking shaken, but Olivier had done all the nasty work. "Do you think it was your disgruntled artist?" he questioned her.

"I can't think of anyone else who would do a crazy thing like that." It had been disgusting. Olivier had taken photographs with his phone in case she wanted to report it to the police, but there was no way to know who had done it, and there were no surveillance cameras in her building. The guardian didn't work on Saturdays, so no one could have seen the culprit, and someone had obviously let him into the building without being buzzed in. She guessed that he must have waited until someone went out, and slipped in. The florist box looked harmless enough, so no one had stopped him.

When they had finished cleaning up, thrown all the debris away, and scrubbed themselves thoroughly, Olivier looked at Amanda with tender concern.

"Let's go for a drive. You need to get out of here." She was deathly pale again, as she had been the night Olivier told her he was married. She had had a traumatic couple of weeks, and he felt guilty for his part in it. She didn't deserve this. She was a good person, and he could see that she was frightened as she went to put on clean jeans and a sweater for a ride to anywhere, just to get out of the house for a little while. He was glad he had called her and so was she. She wouldn't have bothered him otherwise, and she had no idea how she would have cleaned up the gory mess herself, the fish was so big and heavy. Olivier guessed it weighed twenty pounds.

They left Lulu in the kitchen where they had put her so she didn't get into the area that had been cleaned, and twenty minutes later, they were on the highway, heading toward Normandy. Amanda started to relax slowly as they drove along, and the suburbs soon turned to countryside with farms and cottages and farm animals grazing. She could feel the tension go out of her body, as they drove and spoke from time to time. It was peaceful being there with him, and the ugly incident from the morning faded slowly from their minds, as the bucolic countryside took over.

They stopped for lunch at a country inn Olivier knew, and he had her laughing by the end of the meal, but then she grew serious again.

"Tell me about your sons. You've never told me anything about them." Now that they were no longer a secret, she wanted to know about them, and their relationship with him.

"We were very close when they were growing up. Less so now, since they live far away, especially Guillaume in Argentina. He loves it, unfortunately. I don't think he'll ever come back to live in France again. And now he's seriously involved with a woman there." Olivier spoke in a nostalgic tone about both boys, and she could tell he was a dedicated father. "My younger son, Edouard, is more like me. He's gregarious and loves to have fun. He was a ski-racing champion in his teens. He's the one who lives in Switzerland. He's still young, and Geneva is quite near. I go skiing with him when I can get away. I'm no match for him anymore. He goes like the wind. And I don't want to break anything." Olivier was only forty-seven and she could tell he was in good condition. "Do you ski?" he asked her.

"Only if I have to." She smiled. "I don't want to break anything either, and I've never been a great skier. My real talent is après-ski. Velvet stretch pants, Cristal champagne, a little caviar. Put me by the fire and I'm all set."

"Actually, that sounds very appealing," he commented, and glanced at her with a smile.

They headed back to the city after lunch and went to her apartment. He was going to collect his cleaning materials and wanted to check the smell in the apartment. They had left the windows open, and it was completely gone. Only the damp spot on the hall carpet with a faint chemical odor remained. He had done an impeccable job. "I used to fish as a boy, and I always made a mess. My mother made me clean it up, so I have a bit of experience. That was a hell of a nasty fish they gave you," he said, admiring her apartment. He hadn't had time to look around thoroughly before. She had a collection of eclectic objects from her travels, which fascinated him. Masks and fossils, and handcrafted boxes, some sculptures from Africa, and two splendid white beaded chairs from Nigeria that looked like thrones.

"You have some wonderful things, Amanda," he said admiringly.

"Too many," she said, pointing at a bookcase full of beautiful objects, with some delicate blown glass from Italy. "I love finding odd things to bring home when I travel."

"Do you travel a lot?" He was still getting to know her and loved everything he saw and heard.

"Not anymore. Only to find new artists now, or to visit the ones we have. I used to spend a lot of time in Africa and India when I was younger. I've done that, I don't need to go back anymore. It's not easy travel, and some of the areas I loved are politically dangerous now. The world has changed."

"I wish I had done more of that when I was younger," he said. "I was tied down with the boys. My wife was always at a horse show somewhere. She tried to get me into it in the beginning, but I've never liked horses. They're just big dumb animals to me, which is sacrilege to her. She goes to all the shows with her women friends now. A lot of women like riding and all the equestrian events. The people involved in it are a special breed. And they all know each other. I liked hunting and fishing when I was younger. Now I hunt for talented young writers, like you with your artists."

"Do you ever think of writing yourself?"

He smiled when she asked him, over a glass of wine as they sat on the couch in her elegant living room. He liked the way she decorated, and the way she mixed different styles of art. "I've actually written two very boring nonfiction books, about the psychology of the creative arts and the different ways it's expressed. I used to dream of writing a novel, but I don't think I have the talent or the imagination for it."

"I'll bet you could write one if you tried," she said, and he smiled.

It was peaceful being with her. Lulu was curled up on her lap sound asleep, and the drive in the country had relaxed them both. Olivier had talked to Amanda about his parents that afternoon. They had been typical, boring, snobbish aristocrats, according to him. He had a brother who had died in a car accident at eighteen, and his parents were gone now too. He had no family except his wife and his two sons. She wondered if that was part of why he hadn't divorced. He had been educated in France and Switzerland. He described it as a very predictable life ruled by tradition. Amanda was much more adventuresome than he was.

"I've always wanted to go to Wyoming, ever since I was a boy."

"It's very beautiful, the mountains there are very mysterious. I went to a dude ranch with my mother once. It was a lot of fun. I wish I had done more with her. We never know how short or long we will have people for, and I was a rebellious teenager in the two years we had alone."

Night fell as they were talking, exchanging poignant memories of the past, and the kind of things you don't say at a dinner party, and only to close friends. Amanda was surprised by how late it had gotten while they talked. It was after eight o'clock, and she was about to suggest cooking dinner for him, when he leaned over and kissed her, and all the confidences they had shared ignited a passion that nothing could hold back. They were both desperate as they found their way to her bedroom and consummated the desire they had felt for each other since they reconnected, two months after they first met. And now he was forbidden fruit since she knew he was married, which made their lovemaking even more exquisite since the love they shared was fragile now and only borrowed. They lay breathless on her bed afterward. It had been an incredible blending of bodies and souls.

"Wow!" Olivier said, as he rolled onto his side to look at her and drifted a fingertip down her perfect body. "You are an extraordinary woman, Amanda Delanoe." He leaned down to kiss her. "Why did we wait so long?"

"I'm glad we did." They knew each other now, and what they were getting into, and despite her misgivings about his marital status, she had no regrets. She had cast her lot with his now. She knew his situation and she was leery of it and didn't like it, but she was in love with him. She had no idea where fate would take them next, but she had signed on for the journey now, with her eyes and heart wide open. He kissed her then, and made love to her again. The second time was even better than the first.

Chapter 7

Olivier and Amanda slept peacefully in each other's arms that night after they made love. They had eaten dinner at nearly midnight, some pasta they found in a kitchen cupboard and a salad she made from what was in the fridge.

"I eat out a lot," she explained, "or I order in. I'm not very interested in cooking," she confessed with a grin.

"I used to cook for my kids, just basic stuff, when their mother was traveling," which sounded like most of the time. "I didn't mind her traveling because I got to know my sons that way. I never missed a practice or a sports game." Olivier was proud of it, she could tell. "You never wanted children?" he asked, surprised. She had a nurturing side.

"I was never with the right man," she said honestly. "And I wasn't brave enough to do it alone. That didn't look like fun. I didn't want a child enough to raise one on my own. And time got away from me.

When you're young, you think you'll be young forever, and then suddenly you're not."

"You are. You could still have a child if you wanted one."

"I hope not." She laughed. "Besides, it would upset Lulu too much. She's my first child. I've never felt any pressure about getting married or having children. Maybe losing my parents so young taught me that you don't have anyone forever, no matter how much you love them. And children only stay with you for such a short time." He nodded. She was very wise.

"I discovered that when both my boys left the same year. Maybe that's part of why Stephanie and I stay married," he said, thinking about it. "She has a sister she doesn't speak to. Both her parents are alive, with severe Alzheimer's, and they're very old now. My brother and my parents died. Our boys are grown up and gone. We're the only family for each other now. We hardly see each other, but we know that if something happens, the other one will be around to pick up the pieces, or at least send someone to help. She's not a nurturer, but she's responsible and very organized, and so am I. We've never had a warm relationship." Amanda was far warmer and more loving than his wife, which he found touching. "But we're people others can count on." Amanda had discovered that yesterday with the fish. "That's worth something, I suppose," he said.

Amanda had made him accountable for why he had stayed married to a woman he hadn't been in love with for almost their entire marriage. It was practical, if nothing else, which seemed like a poor excuse not to divorce, even to him. He couldn't actually explain why he had stayed married to Stephanie, except that he felt it was the right thing to do, and it was expected of him. He had never questioned that for twenty-six years, until he met Amanda, and now things had changed. He was stuck with a life and a woman that didn't suit him, and he had seriously upset the woman he had fallen in love with. But it was all still very new. He was grateful she was giving him and their relationship a chance. It was brave of her and made him love her more.

Things were subtly different too now that they had made love. It provided an invisible bond between them, a kind of glue that he and his wife had never had. They had stopped having sex entirely twenty-four years before, after Edouard was conceived. It was amazing what people settled for by tacit agreement, without ever saying a word.

Amanda had had one late call from a blocked number shortly after midnight, while they were cleaning up after dinner. She guessed immediately that it would be the breather. No one ever called her at that hour. She looked frightened and didn't answer it. Olivier picked up the receiver and spoke into it in a strong male tone.

"We know who you are and we're going to call the police," he said. "Don't call here again," and then he disconnected the call. There were no further calls that night. It was useful having a man around, and Lulu didn't object to him as much as Amanda had feared. She wagged her tail a few times in his direction, got into one of her beds, and went to sleep. Amanda didn't put her in bed with them that night.

They went out for breakfast on Sunday morning, to a little place Olivier knew that made delicious omelets, and then they took a long walk along the river. The city was quiet and peaceful, and he stayed with her until that night, and then he went back to his own place. He had told her that Stephanie was at a horse show in Deauville that weekend, with her friends. She was coming home for a night, and then leaving for England for a series of events there.

"I'm going to talk to her eventually, but not when she's home for one night on the fly. And it's too soon." Amanda agreed with him. She wanted him to *be* divorced, but didn't want to be the cause of it, whom everyone would blame. It had to come from him because he wanted it. Then they could have a real life together. But he did seem to have as much freedom as he said. Amanda wondered if his wife had had a man in her life for all these years, maybe someone in her horse world. It didn't seem as though Olivier would have cared. Or at least not this late in the day. And now he had Amanda. Their marriage seemed to her a sad way to live. Strangers living under the same roof occasionally, like guests in a hotel.

The apartment seemed strangely quiet after he left. He wasn't a noisy person, and he didn't make a mess. But he was a strong male presence which made itself felt. And his absence was equally noticeable. After recent events, the calls and the gutted fish, she felt safer and protected somehow when he was around.

She caught up on reading some art magazines on Sunday night and watched part of a series on TV. She looked rested and relaxed when she got to the gallery on Monday. Pascal noticed it immediately but didn't comment about it at first.

"What did you do this weekend?" he asked her casually. "After you got rid of the dead fish. That sounded disgusting, by the way."

"It was," she confirmed. "I took a drive in the country, went for a walk along the Seine, and went out for breakfast on Sunday." Pascal was smiling by then. None of those things were activities she would have done alone, and he could guess easily who she was with.

"Did Olivier spend the night?"

"Funny you should ask. What makes you say that?"

"I know you. You don't go driving to the country, walk along the Seine, or go out for breakfast on your own. You look like you've had a two-week vacation, by the way. He's good for you."

"I think he is. I still don't like his situation, but he seems to be as free as he says. She was in Deauville this weekend, at a horse show. It might be different when she's home. We'll see. She doesn't come home much. His description of his marriage is out of a bad book. It's sad to stay married like that."

"A lot of people do. They settle for what they get, and then go looking for other people to make it work. Be careful, though, they may have one set of rules for when she's away, and another set for when she's at home."

"Not according to him, but you may be right. You seem to know more about all this than I do. I always thought married was married, except for my father. But all he ever wanted were pretty girls for the night. I think my mother was the main event, as much as he was capable of it. It's too bad he screwed it up. She deserved a better deal than she got. She was so good to him, and she really loved him. She never forgave him once she found out, and then the roof caved in, and she left. What's happening with you by the way? How's the little artist?"

"Delphine finally agreed to go out with me. I've taken her to dinner seven times so far. She hasn't slept with me yet. She says I'm a slut, and she wants a serious relationship with a serious guy. I'm thinking of cleaning up my act. Maybe. And now she wants a dog like Lulu."

Amanda laughed. "Watch out. She's just the kind of girl who'll get you one day."

"She's pretty amazing. She's really smart. And a good artist. She won a prize at the Venice Biennale last year."

"That's impressive." Amanda was more impressed that Delphine was trying to tame Pascal and hadn't slept with him yet. She had definitely gotten his attention by doing that. He was used to women falling at his feet, and into his bed.

Amanda worked hard at the gallery until Thursday night. Then she and Olivier left for the promised weekend at the borrowed house in Saint-Tropez. It was a beautiful home, with a cook, two maids, and a butler, who waited on them very discreetly. They explored the shops in town, had drinks in the port, and admired the yachts. They had dinner at the Caves du Roy, and then danced until three A.M. They lay by the pool at the house in total luxury and privacy. It was like a honeymoon.

With his wife out of town almost all the time, it was easy to forget that Olivier was married. He didn't seem like he was, and didn't feel that way either. He acted like a free man.

He introduced Amanda to people he knew, and they had drinks on the yacht of a friend of his, who had a woman with him who was not his wife either. She was about to leave on Sunday, when the friend's wife was coming down to join him on the yacht. It was a very different world for Amanda, this world of women who were not married to the men they traveled and slept with, and who knew they were married to someone else. It was a whole subculture she had been unaware of before and never thought about. She didn't like being considered part of it, and so far she wasn't open about it, but she was there in a front-row seat, which made her one of them, like it or not. It didn't seem respectable to her.

They went back to Paris on Sunday night, and he stayed with her. Stephanie was out of town, although he still insisted nothing would change when she was back.

While they were in Saint-Tropez, Amanda told him she had been invited to an art show in Venice, and asked if he wanted to go, and he said he couldn't when she told him the date.

"Both boys are coming home that weekend. They haven't been home in ages. It's their mother's birthday. And I should be around. I want to see my sons. They only come home once or twice a year now, especially Guillaume from Buenos Aires."

It was the first weekend that he wouldn't be with her, and his wife would be in town, and the children. It suddenly made Amanda feel left out, knowing he would be with them. He obviously wanted to spend time with his sons, but it was going to be family time for him. He had been generous with his time with her, but knowing he was going to spend a whole weekend with his family, she felt a flutter of butterflies in her stomach. She was jealous of his being with them. They were his family, and Stephanie was his wife, with all the dignity that entailed, and Amanda felt like the woman/"slut" that he was sleeping with. She didn't like the job title, although she was sure that she was closer to Olivier than his wife was, by far.

The rest of the time, she and Olivier forgot that he was married. They had a full and busy life and went to a number of events together. He introduced her to everyone with no explanation. She didn't need one. It was a world where relationships like theirs were commonplace and came with a multitude of perks, like a fancy Mercedes or the Bentley sport model. Clothes and jewelry, and alligator Birkins with diamond clasps. Amanda wanted none of those from him, or anything for that matter. She had everything she needed. She was more like his wife than a mistress when they traveled together, and so far his marital status hadn't interfered with them at all.

It was very different from the relationship she'd had previously with the married man who'd hidden her in cheap motels and lived in fear of being discovered by his wife. Olivier was a much nicer person and he saw to it that Amanda was always respected, comfortable, and treated well.

When Olivier went home to get ready for his sons' visit, Amanda planned to get caught up on things she couldn't do when he was around: she wanted to do some reading, tidy her closets, have dinner with some of her artists. She was going to work the following weekend. She and Pascal had a show to hang, the weekends were the best time to do it, and she'd be busy while Olivier was with his kids.

Tom called her on Sunday night and asked if she could have dinner with him the following weekend. He said the writing was going well, but he was going to take a break from the book and wanted to see her, and she told him she couldn't. She said she was going to hang a show with Pascal, which was always a big undertaking. They usually worked on hanging their shows until midnight for several nights.

Tom sounded a little miffed in his response when she said she was busy the next weekend, which told her he hadn't made any friends yet, but was working on his book and not going out.

It was also a wake-up call to her when she realized that she was jealous of the time Olivier was going to spend with his family. It was a reminder that he was in fact married, and there were other people who were important to him in his life, and a priority. But other than that, he had been with her almost constantly and rarely spent a night at home. Pascal wondered if Olivier's wife knew he slept out so frequently, and if she'd react to it, but she hadn't so far. Stephanie was constantly traveling to dressage shows with her horses, just as Olivier had said in the beginning. And he seemed to be as free and available as he had claimed.

Amanda still got occasional odd calls late at night, which she assumed were the breather. He called but much less frequently. Olivier answered the phone at night, in a stern tone, and sometimes as soon as the caller heard a male voice, he hung up.

Olivier didn't like that she still got those calls, and had suggested changing her number, which was a nuisance she didn't want to bother with. And she guessed that the caller was a random stranger who had picked her number. They'd had no direct contact from Johnny Vegas, who Pascal had heard was back in rehab. But someone was still calling her from time to time. Johnny Vegas hadn't shown up at the gallery to threaten them for dropping him from their roster of artists. He had even sent them a letter of apology, to make amends. It was part of his current rehab program, so Amanda and Pascal didn't anticipate any further problems with him, unless he left rehab and started shooting heroin again. They were sorry he was wasting his talent, and hoped he'd clean up, although they didn't want to represent him again, which he seemed to understand and accept.

Olivier was fascinated by the business, and loved what Amanda taught him about contemporary art. She always had something to show him, or a story to tell him. She included him in her world, when he had time. He was never bored with her. And he occasionally gave her good advice about her business.

He didn't invade her space, and she loved including him in it. And Lulu got excited now whenever she saw him. Amanda had given Olivier a closet, and he kept some things at her apartment so he could dress for dinner, or go straight to work, and have casual clothes for the weekend. He felt totally at home in her apartment and had settled in quickly. They had gotten used to each other.

She was sad when he left on Sunday night, two days before his sons were due to arrive. Stephanie was due home on Sunday, a few hours before Olivier kissed Amanda and left. The silence seemed a little worse to Amanda because she knew Stephanie would be there when he went home. She knew it was foolish to be jealous of her. Amanda had the best part of Olivier, but it bothered her anyway, and she sounded glum when Tom called her that night to invite her to dinner and she reminded him that she was hanging a show with Pascal. "How's the book coming?"

"It's exciting," he said, "I've created the most intriguing murders. No one is going to figure out who the murderer is until the last page," he added, gloating.

"That sounds terrifying," she said with a laugh.

"It is. It's hard to keep it all together, and make sure all the loopholes are filled. Is *he* there?" he asked. She didn't know who he was talking about.

"Who?" She thought he might mean Pascal.

"Olivier, your boyfriend."

Amanda felt a little silly referring to him as that, since they were adults. "No, why?"

"I just wondered. Is he living with you now?" She didn't want to answer his questions. It was none of his business.

"I'm quite alone, thank you," she said stiffly. "What about you? Have you met any nice women yet?"

"No, I've been writing. That's why I'm here. And not speaking French is a handicap trying to meet women in bars."

"Maybe you should take a quick Berlitz class. But a lot of women speak English here, and there are all the foreigners: the Brits, the Dutch, the Scandinavians, the Germans. They all speak English."

"I've been busy. I'll let you know when I take another break from the book. I'm sorry I forgot you were busy this weekend. I lose track of everything when I write."

"Good luck," she said sincerely, but she didn't like the edge in his voice when he asked about Olivier, and sometimes even Pascal. Tom still had a jealous streak, and was bitter about his divorce. He hated his ex-wife, which didn't help his attitude about women. She wondered if that came through when he tried to meet new ones.

She went back to her desk after Tom called and forgot about him quickly. She made notes for the show they were going to hang that weekend, but found it hard to concentrate. Her mind kept rolling back to Olivier, at his home with his wife. Despite everything he had told her about his loveless marriage, knowing he was there with her was a knife in her heart. She had lived through that before and didn't like being there again. It was a bad déjà vu for her, and brought back painful memories.

Chapter 8

Pascal and Amanda closed the gallery two hours early on Friday evening to start hanging the show, and were going to finish the installation on Saturday. It was a big show, with a lot of work and huge canvases, which was challenging and fun to do, to figure out how best to showcase each painting. It took them two days to hang a show that size. They had two young men with them to hold the work up for them to adjust heights and lighting. It was going to be a big job, and Amanda had been making notes about it all week. She laid it out on the floor first and showed it to Pascal, and he suggested some changes they tried out, and she liked them. They worked well together, and each contributed to the look of the show.

"I love this guy's work, don't you? I love his brushwork, his palette, the way he takes over the canvas," Pascal said. The artist had rapidly become successful in the past two years, and they were excited to be showing his work and wanted to hang it well. He had recently signed with them.

Once they locked the doors, they had paintings leaning against all the walls, and Amanda had made diagrams, which she was still playing with, to show the work at its best possible advantage. It took concentration and a sense of balance to put the right pieces next to each other. And the large paintings were cumbersome to get up on the walls. The men helping them were tired after three hours up and down ladders. Pascal was helping one of them with the lighting.

A lot went into hanging their shows. Pascal always said that Amanda had an unfailing eye, and they made a number of changes and decisions as they carefully hung each piece.

They stopped for half an hour around nine-thirty that night to eat a slice of pizza, while observing what they'd done with a critical eye. They switched two paintings around.

"I like the red one there, do you?" Amanda asked Pascal. "People will see it as soon as they walk in, and it will knock them on their asses. I'll bet we sell it in the first hour," she said, looking pleased with what they'd hung, and Pascal agreed with her on every placement so far. They loved working together and agreed the show was going to be a hit.

They were wrestling with the biggest canvas in the show at midnight. It took two of them to hold it, and two to hang it. They had to set it down several times and try again before they got it placed to Amanda's satisfaction. But it was perfect when they did. The piece was spectacular: a red background, heavy black brushstrokes, Chinese characters integrated into the design, a bold swath of royal blue with a circle of yellow. Amanda was going to place a large red sculpture near it to enhance it. She looked like a kid in a candy factory. She grinned at Pascal when they got the biggest piece right, and he smiled at her. She loved the work they did. They built the rest of the show around the main painting to complement it and balance the show.

"God, I love that piece," she said, and sat down on a chair to admire it.

"I love the way you love what we do," he said happily. The show was already looking great, and it wasn't even half hung. "Do you want to call it a night?" he asked her.

"Why don't we do one more? It'll be that much less to do tomorrow, and we're on a roll." He nodded, agreeing with her. He liked hanging the shows at night when they had no distractions, and no one wandering around the gallery. The rest of the pieces were slightly smaller, so they would be easier to hang. In the end they hung two more pieces, which looked perfect together and strengthened each other. They stopped at one-thirty in the morning, with half the show left to hang on Saturday. The opening was on Monday. Pascal had to photograph the show once it was up.

They were admiring their work when the two young men left, promising to be back at ten the next morning. Pascal and Amanda were closing the gallery on Saturday, so they could finish hanging.

"Where's Olivier this weekend?" Pascal asked her, as he put their tools away neatly. He was surprised he wasn't with Amanda, and hadn't dropped by. Olivier liked hanging around the gallery and being with her whenever possible. He was a frequent visitor and admired the work they showed. He was learning a lot about it from Amanda.

"He's at home," she said quietly, in answer to his question.

"Home at your place, or his?" Pascal could see that Amanda was upset about something. He thought maybe she and Olivier had had an argument, although it had been smooth sailing so far, according to her, and most of the time she looked ecstatic when his name was mentioned.

"His. His boys flew in this week for their mother's birthday. She got back on Sunday from some horse show or other. With the boys back, he wanted to be at home this week so he'd have time with them. He thought it would look better to everyone if he stayed there and didn't make waves or bring attention to himself. He claims she doesn't care where he is, but he was definite about being with his family this week."

"And you're upset about it?" Pascal quizzed her. It was easy to see she was. Amanda turned to look at him then and he could see the pain in her eyes.

"I thought I'd be fine, and he always tells me he's totally free. But the reality is he's married, and I've gotten used to having him around. It hit me like a wrecking ball after he left. I've been sick about it all week. What if he's more attached to her than he admits? Or she objects to his sleeping out anymore? We're at his wife's mercy and what she'll put up with. Maybe he's unrealistic about how free he really is."

"Have you heard from him?" Pascal asked.

"He's been calling two or three times a day, but he's busy. He can't talk much, and he's working and staying there at night to be with his boys. I don't want to bother him, but all I can think about is that he's with her this week, and not with me. I hate this situation. And he's so generous with his time, I can't complain to him. He's trying to meet everyone's needs. Hers, mine, his sons'. It was always bound to be hard at times, but it's harder than I thought. And he doesn't like talking on the phone from that house. He never knows who's listening. It feels like shit having him there. I hate it. It makes me feel like I'm a second-class citizen and I don't matter."

"Of course you matter. More than she does," Pascal reassured her.

"That's what he *says,* but who knows if that's the truth? I feel like an adulterer again. It's just the way it is."

"I'm sorry."

"Yeah, me too. And I don't want to complain to him. He's doing the best he can to keep everyone happy. And he's so good to me. He really is a wonderful person."

"So are you," Pascal said gently, then looked at something past her shoulder, through the picture window. She saw him react and was startled.

"Did you see something?" she asked him.

"I thought I did. It's probably an illusion or a reflection. I thought I saw a guy watching us, wearing a beanie and a face mask. Like a science fiction movie." They both stared through the picture window and saw nothing. "I must have imagined it. I'm seeing things." Pascal stuck his head out the front door before locking it again. There was no sign of movement anywhere on the street. "That's so weird. It looked so real." And then he remembered something.

"Someone told me today that Johnny Vegas is out of rehab. They weren't absolutely sure, but they thought so. They heard a rumor. That would be bad news if he is, if he's still pissed at us for firing him."

"I'm sure he isn't. We didn't put him in rehab." They'd been told by another artist it had been court-ordered.

"Yeah, he really is a mess. I hope he isn't out yet, and I don't want him showing up at this show and making trouble. It will frighten the clients and the artist."

"He wouldn't have the nerve," Amanda said with assurance.

"He might. Let's pray to the gods of rehab that they didn't let him out. That would be a big mistake. Huge," Pascal said seriously. He didn't like guys on drugs hanging around the gallery, risking that they'd damage the art. The gallery had insurance, but art was irreplaceable. Each piece was unique.

Pascal checked the front door again before they left, and they walked out the back door, double-locked it, and set the alarm. He gave Amanda a ride home. It was almost two A.M. by then.

When Olivier came home from Amanda's on Sunday evening, Stephanie had already arrived from the horse show she'd been to in Dordogne that weekend. She had dropped her horses off at the stable where she kept them and got them settled. There were three stable hands hired to drive the trailers, as well as exercise the horses between shows. Stephanie and her three friends had driven into the city together, in the SUV they always rode in, which belonged to Stephanie. Olivier had bought it for her. On the drive back to Paris, they talked about the results of the show that weekend. Two of the women had done well. The third had had a disappointing showing with a horse she was trying out, and wasn't fully trained yet. It had been his first show.

"He's just a baby," Valerie said in a forgiving tone. "He has a long way to go." The four women had done the show circuit together for the past twenty years. Some of some of them had been barely more than kids themselves then. It was their passion, and they were top-notch riders. Stephanie and Lizzie ranked in the top ten in France, Valerie and Veronique in the top twenty.

Stephanie was the strongest rider of the four. She was a tall, thin dark-haired woman, not a beauty, but she had grown into her looks as she got older. At forty-seven, she could be called handsome. For the shows, she wore her dark brown hair in a tight bun, at other times she wore it down, to her shoulders. She was a no-frills person, dressed simply, and wore very little makeup, just a touch of lipstick in a neutral tone. Her closest friend in the group was Elizabeth Bonnard, a petite redhead with a personality to match her hair. She was lively and fun. Veronique and Valerie were slightly portly blondes. They had gone to school together and almost looked like twins. The three women had known each other since their early twenties, and Lizzie was ten years younger. They were the senior pros of the show circuit, and entered dressage shows and jumping competitions all over Europe. Veronique and Valerie had both been married briefly and divorced, and neither one had children. Lizzie had never been married or had kids. She and Stephanie were inseparable and Lizzie worshipped Stephanie. Stephanie had taught her how to perfect her jumping skills and show techniques. Lizzie was thirty-eight. Veronique and Valerie were approaching fifty, and Stephanie was forty-seven.

"Will Olivier be home?" Lizzie asked her, and Stephanie said she assumed he would. The boys were due in on Tuesday, and her birthday was the following weekend.

"It'll be nice to see the boys," Stephanie said, and smiled at Lizzie.

"What are you going to do this week?" They were taking the week off while they were home. The horses would be exercised every day.

"Sleep," Lizzie said with a mischievous grin. Preparing for the shows was grueling. Veronique and Valerie had families who helped to pay their expenses and could afford to, and Olivier paid for Stephanie's. Lizzie's family didn't assist her, but Stephanie had helped her protégée for years. It was an expensive sport, but for all four of them, it was their first love and their passion.

They had been on the road for a month from show to show and had done particularly well in Italy and England. And they'd done well in Dordogne and Périgord that weekend too.

Stephanie dropped them all off at their homes in the city, where they all lived. Valerie and Veronique shared an apartment, and Lizzie had a studio not far from Stephanie's house. It was convenient when they got together to discuss which shows they wanted to enter, and they had plans to go to the States that summer, to enter shows in North Carolina and Virginia. Lizzie had done well there the year before.

When Stephanie got home, she drove her car into the garage and saw that Olivier wasn't home yet. She had spoken to him last week, to make plans for the boys' visit. She hadn't seen him in weeks, and her sons in four months. It was hard to find time for a personal life with all the training and traveling they did. All four of the women rode every day.

Stephanie was in the kitchen eating a sandwich when Olivier walked in. He looked at her in surprise and didn't approach her. He knew how much she hated being embraced. She had a cool, distant nature, like a wild horse.

"You're home. How did the show go yesterday?" he asked pleasantly.

"We did well. I got first, Lizzie second, the other girls didn't do as well, third and fourth in another category." Olivier knew it was the only language she spoke and the only thing she cared about, other than their sons. He wasn't on her radar most of the time.

"Congratulations. You must be tired," he said, and poured himself a glass of wine. Stephanie already had one. With Amanda to compare it to now, he was startled to realize how bloodless their relationship was. There were no hugs or embraces, no visible pleasure to be seeing each other again. They used to talk about their children, now they talked more about her shows and horses. They shared no personal information, and behaved like strangers even after she'd been gone for a month. They hadn't shared a bedroom in years. Stephanie used to say Olivier's snoring kept her up at night, and they were both relieved when they gave up the pretense of sharing a room a few years after Edouard's birth.

Stephanie had a lithe, athletic build, and worked out every morning. She was most at ease in her riding habits. She had admitted to her friends that she felt like a freak now in a dress. She claimed to have knobby knees and bony legs, and she was tall enough that she never had to wear high heels. She said she couldn't walk in them anyway.

She had been a tomboy as a child, with three brothers. She could run faster than they could, climbed trees better, and was a better rider now. All of her family were avid horsemen. It was all they talked about. Olivier had thought she'd outgrow it, or be less interested in horses once she married and they had children, but she hadn't. And her riding world bored him to tears. He had thought her athletic prowess was sexy when they were young, but it was less so now. He had no illusions, she was stronger than he was and could do a hundred pushups on one hand. He could barely make it through ten, or five, with both hands. Gymnastics had never been his strong suit, and he hated going to the gym. But fortunately he didn't need to, and was naturally in good shape with a minimum of exercise. He played tennis once a week. Tennis bored Stephanie as much as horses did him.

Olivier sometimes wondered how they had fallen in love, or if they really had. He'd been shy as a boy and was friends with her brothers, and she was always hanging around competing with them, so when he first got interested in girls, she was close at hand and easy to talk to. He knew her well and he didn't have to make much effort with her, having known her since they were children.

Their families were enthusiastic about the match, and the next thing he knew they were married, and he realized it was like marrying one of the guys. They were both inept at sex, had both been virgins, and had no idea what to do with each other. He thought having a baby might bring them closer, but it didn't. She hated being pregnant and not being able to ride for several months, and once the baby was born, Olivier took care of Guillaume more than Stephanie did. But she was relieved it was a boy. She talked about teaching him to ride one day. Until then, he was Olivier's baby.

The first time he cheated on her was after Edouard was born. A beautiful young woman moved in next door to them, and he suddenly realized that women were a great deal more alluring if they didn't act like one of the guys. He was twenty-four years old, had been married for three years and had two children, and the neighbor was twenty-two and had a body like a Playboy model. There had been many girls like her after that, until he finally settled down in his thirties and became more discriminating. He and Stephanie had never had sex after Edouard was conceived. He was disappointed and embarrassed about it at first, until he realized that Stephanie was relieved. She didn't want to get pregnant again and had developed an aversion to sex. Any time he approached her, she had an excuse. The sexy girl next door was much more willing. She was the first of many partners he had in his twenties. He was surprised to find that other women found him attractive, even though his wife didn't.

"Where were you today?" she asked him when he got home. It was Sunday. He had come straight from Amanda's, and had made love to her before he left her.

"I stopped by to see a friend. I meant to get back earlier. We were watching a football match," which meant soccer in France. She nodded and didn't ask him anything else. She didn't know his friends anyway, or like the few she knew.

They had dinner together in the kitchen on Monday night. They each cooked their own meal and conversation was sparse. He was distracted. Amanda texted him a few times and he didn't stop her, and before they left the kitchen, Stephanie gave him a knowing look.

"You've got someone new again, don't you? You always get that starry-eyed look. It makes you look like a kid again." It was a statement more than a criticism. She was never jealous, acting more like a sister or a friend than a wife.

"Is that a compliment or an accusation?" he asked her, and didn't answer her question. He never did. They shared no details about their lives.

"Neither one. More of an observation. Someone decent, I hope."

"What does that mean?" He bristled at her comment.

"Just someone who won't make trouble, or blackmail you, or put you in an embarrassing position and try to extort money from you."

"When did I ever get blackmailed?" he asked her, annoyed.

"It can happen. Men are drawn to women like that like flies to honey. We don't need a scandal," she said. She and her family were very conservative and proper.

"You won't have one," he said simply, and walked out of the kitchen, leaving his plate in the sink, and went upstairs to his room. Just seeing Stephanie made him miss Amanda, and he realized now how right she was, about how pointless it was to stay married to someone you didn't love, just to avoid a divorce. What they had wasn't a marriage and never had been. It had been a travesty, but they had stayed married anyway. It was the only victory they could claim. It depressed him to think about it, and he lay down on his bed and called Amanda again. He had closed his bedroom door before he did.

"How's it going?" she asked him. He didn't mention Stephanie's comment. He wondered how she always knew that he had met a woman he liked. Most of them didn't last long, but this one would. For twenty-three years, until now, it had always been purely physical. Amanda was different. He was in love with her.

By the end of the week, he and his wife had run out of even minor conversation with each other. The boys were leaving on Sunday, after their mother's birthday, and all Olivier wanted was to go back to Amanda's arms and bed. He had stuck around more than usual all week because of the boys, but even they seemed eager to leave. Their home was a hollow shell with no love in it, or too little. Olivier felt love-starved by the end of the week. And he wondered if Stephanie felt that way too. Her friends were in and out of the house every day. He would hear them talking and laughing in the kitchen, but they felt awkward around him and fell silent the minute he walked in. He felt like an intruder in their midst. It had been a hard week for all of them. The whole horse group was leaving for England soon, and all he wanted was to spend the night with Amanda. He knew he could spend the night out while his wife was there, but he didn't want his sons to notice it, or have it cause comment. He had always tried to set an example for them, of being a responsible and respectable family man. They admired Olivier, and he didn't want to disappoint them and show his needs and flaws to them. It made their relationship less real, but he felt he had a role to play in front of them, without letting his failings show. Stephanie did the same, although Guillaume and Edouard knew their parents' relationship wasn't warm. He could wait a few more days, and then Stephanie would be gone. Then he could go home to Amanda and bask in the warmth of the love she lavished on him. It had become familiar to him, and he needed Amanda like air to breathe, and nourishment. He had been starved before he met her.

Amanda was almost falling asleep on the way back to her apartment after the first night of hanging the show. She couldn't wait to get to bed, and to finish installing it the next day. Pascal dropped her off in front of her building, and watched her go in. Once the outer door closed behind her, she ran up the stairs to her apartment, unlocked the front door, and walked in. She hadn't bothered to put the alarm on. The building was safe. There hadn't been a robbery in the building in all the years she'd lived there.

She walked into her bedroom to find Lulu and saw that the bedroom door and window were wide open, her closet door was open, and the light was on, and it suddenly clicked that someone had been in her apartment, and possibly still was. She grabbed Lulu and her keys, with her phone still in her pocket, and ran out the front door of the apartment and down the stairs, out of the building and onto the street. And from there she called the police and told them that her apartment had been burglarized, and she thought the burglar might still be inside. She didn't want to ask Pascal to come back, they were both so tired, so she called Olivier. He was awake in his room, reading, and grabbed his cellphone immediately, as soon as he saw it was her.

"Are you okay?" he asked her. It was unlike her to call him so late.

"No, yes. I'm fine, but my apartment has been burglarized."

"Is Lulu okay?"

"She's fine. I grabbed her and ran and called the police from the street. They said they'd be here in ten minutes." As she said it, she could hear the police siren approaching, and saw the flashing blue lights a minute later.

"I'll be right there," Olivier said hastily. He got up, put on jeans and a sweater, slipped his feet into loafers, grabbed a jacket and his phone, wallet, and car keys, and ran down the stairs and out of the house. Everyone was sound asleep, and no one heard him drive away.

He was at her front door in fifteen minutes. The police had just checked the apartment, and said that there was no intruder in it, and they asked her to come upstairs and see if she could tell what was missing. She followed them upstairs and Olivier went with her. He kissed her, thrilled to see her. He had dropped by the gallery briefly several times that week, but hadn't spent the night with her, because of his sons.

The police had already determined that one or several intruders had scaled the façade of the building, using the architectural details as handholds, and entered through the now open window. Amanda could see that the glass had been broken and knocked out to facilitate their entry. Her silver cupboard was open, and she thought there were two trays missing that were family heirlooms. Things were knocked over in her bathroom, like perfume bottles and cosmetics. The drawers of the chest were open, and she looked and saw that about half the contents of one of the drawers was missing, and when she looked in the laundry hamper, where some people hid jewelry, the police explained, it was empty, and her dirty laundry was gone. She made a careful tour of the apartment, and forty-five minutes later, all she could tell the police was that a sizable quantity of her underwear and all her dirty laundry was missing, and nothing else. The two silver trays had been left in the kitchen.

"That's crazy!" She stared at them and Olivier. She was still holding Lulu. "Who would take my laundry and my underwear?"

"That's a sexual crime, ma'am," the senior officer informed her. "It's a different department from burglary. That's an erotomaniac, probably a stalker, who may have been watching you. It's not too common, but it happens. It's usually a stranger, someone you don't know or have never noticed." He started to tell her what the culprit would do with the stolen clothing, and she said she didn't want to know. The idea was disgusting, and even more so if someone was stalking her and broke into her home and stole such personal items.

"We'll fill out the report and give it to the right department," the police officer told her. "Get that window fixed quickly, and you need to turn your alarm on next time. The building is vulnerable because of the architectural details. It could happen again, if he likes what he got." She shuddered at the thought, and they left a few minutes later. It was three A.M., and she was exhausted.

"I'm spending the night," Olivier said calmly.

"Can you do that? With her home?" Amanda asked him.

"Of course. I can do whatever I want. She's not going to ask me any questions."

They undressed, went to bed, and talked in the dark about what had happened. It was unnerving, and frightening.

"What if he comes back?" Amanda asked Olivier.

"If I'm here, I'll grab him. But the police were right. You need to use the alarm now." As Olivier said it, the phone rang, and they thought it might be the police. Amanda answered without checking the caller ID, and there was heavy panting at the other end of the line, and it sounded like someone was masturbating or having sex. He was clearly the thief who took her underwear. She disconnected the call immediately, didn't answer when it rang again, and Olivier put his arms around her. He was glad she had called him. There was some very sick guy following her, stalking her. Olivier held her tight, and she was shaking. It took them a long time to fall asleep, and Olivier didn't leave her until she left for work in the morning. He dropped her off at the gallery and made sure that Pascal was there. He had just arrived, and Amanda was late. She told him what had happened, and Olivier kissed her and left them.

"I'll come by tonight," he promised as he left.

"Are you sure? What about your boys? Aren't they leaving tomorrow?" she asked him.

"They're leaving early. I'll say goodbye to them tonight." Stephanie's birthday dinner was that night. "We're having dinner together for the birthday, and I've gotten some good time with both boys this week. They're leaving the house at six A.M. I'll come to you later, after dinner, so keep the alarm on until I get there," he said, and sped away as she explained the details of the situation to Pascal, about the erotomaniac who had broken into her apartment.

"That doesn't sound like Johnny Vegas," Pascal said, worried about her. "It sounds like you picked up a real nutcase." Amanda had brought Lulu to the gallery with her, so she didn't get injured by another intruder. But there was no question that something very nasty was happening to Amanda, and they had no idea who the perpetrator was. It could have been anyone. And if not Johnny Vegas, then who? And most likely, just as the police said, it was someone she didn't know, a total stranger, who was fixated on her. She shuddered, remembering the man panting on the phone. It took her several hours to calm down, until she got engrossed in hanging the show, and tried to forget the pervert who was stalking her while she did.

Chapter 9

Pascal and Amanda went back to work, measuring the space, lighting each painting, and switching them around to achieve a better result when something didn't work. But the memory of her ransacked apartment was disturbing and kept distracting her. It was hard to concentrate. She and Pascal talked about it when they took a break, and the police showed up at lunchtime to interview her. They asked if she had had any romantic liaisons recently which had ended badly, any men she had met recently and rejected sexually, or any strange phone calls. She mentioned the breathing calls she had had for a while now late at night. She hadn't been aware of anyone following her and had had no dates for some time before Olivier. She didn't volunteer his name, since he was married. The stolen underwear and missing laundry were a clear sign to the police that the crime was sexual in nature and that the stalker had fantasies about her.

"You probably don't know him," the police assured her, "and

wouldn't remember if you'd seen him. We get crimes like this with movie stars and models, and ordinary women too, always attractive young women who have very rarely had direct contact with their stalkers. The perpetrators have fantasies about them and can be very persistent, and clever in how they gain access. Keep your windows locked and your alarm on at night," they suggested. "You live alone?" That was usually the case in these minor crimes. They could be very unnerving, but seldom dangerous, although a few led to more violent crimes. The police said that the perpetrators were delusional and often believed that the object of their desires belonged to them, or wanted them, and would welcome their advances, however twisted and unrealistic that was. They often succeeded in breaking into their victims' homes, they told her, so she had to be careful, particularly if she was sleeping alone, and in older buildings where the detailing on the façades made climbing easier. And even in modern buildings, in apartments on the lower floors, or small private homes, they succeeded in entering, and sometimes surprised their victims in their sleep. A few rapes had occurred as a result, and one kidnapping, the senior detective said. The nature of these crimes was not to be taken lightly, but with some good precautions she would be safe, and with no reality to his fantasies and with foiled attempts to connect with her, he would eventually lose interest and move on to another object of his desires. "Some of the men who do this are even married. They have mental problems and can be incredibly persistent. On average it takes about a year to discourage them, sometimes longer. If he tries to make contact with you, don't talk to him, don't tell him to stop, or insist that you're not interested. *Any* contact you have with him will encourage him and feed his delusions. You can tell him no a hundred times, and he'll be convinced you mean yes."

"I have a friend who spends the night with me sometimes," she said, referring to Olivier and again not naming him, not wanting to involve him officially, which could prove awkward for him.

"If he sees a man with you, if he's watching you, it may discourage or slow him down, but it may anger him, because he believes that *he* belongs with you, not the man you have with you."

"It sounds very sick," Amanda said, looking dismayed. And the underwear he had taken was new and expensive, and she had bought it to wear with Olivier.

The police left after half an hour, and Pascal was worried about her. "Will Olivier stay with you for a while now?" he asked her. He didn't like the idea of some nutcase stalking her, nor did Olivier, and she wasn't enjoying it either. It wasn't flattering. It was sick.

The police had said that he might have been watching her for a long time before moving into action and breaking into her apartment, but she had been completely unaware of anyone following her. And they hadn't had any suspicious characters lurking around the gallery, except for Johnny Vegas, but he was there for other reasons, not to claim his "rightful" place with Amanda. He had been furious at having been dismissed as one of their artists, but he had never shown any sexual interest in her. And despite drugs and alcohol, she didn't consider him a pervert. And he was sober and still in rehab now, and sane again. This was obviously a stranger, which made it even more unnerving. She knew no one who would do something like it. She remembered then the one time she'd thought someone was watching her and Olivier when he kissed her good night, but afterward she had decided she'd been paranoid and there was no one.

The police had no current cases similar to hers at the moment, so he wasn't pursuing a number of women, although they said they were going to check the records closely in other arrondissements, and they gave her their standard advice. She'd have to keep her apartment buttoned up tight so he had no access. No doors left open for neighbors, or so the dog could get out, which didn't apply. No open windows on the façade, no unlocked doors on the perimeter of the apartment. And they warned her to be careful with deliveries. He could be artful about wearing a uniform, claiming to be from a delivery service or a store. Since she probably didn't know him, she wouldn't recognize him disguised as a delivery person. It might even have been an artist they didn't know who had come to their openings. She had forgotten to tell them about the dead fish in the florist box, but that appeared to be unrelated, and was right up Johnny Vegas's alley before he went to rehab. What had just happened was much more specific to a sexually related crime, and frightened her because of it. What if he got in again when she was alone and raped her?

Amanda forced the whole incident out of her mind as she and Pascal continued hanging the show, and by the late afternoon it was looking great. She stepped back to look at it with a broad smile, pleased with their work, and Pascal congratulated her. The way they had organized it showed the work to its best advantage, and she was proud of how it looked. The opening on Monday was going to be gorgeous.

Olivier showed up in the late afternoon, and thought it looked terrific too. It amazed him how different the gallery looked with the way they set up each show. Amanda had ordered flowers to coordinate with the artwork to put in two enormous vases at the front of the gallery, near the reception desk, so they would be the first thing people saw when they walked in. She had enormous talent with anything visual.

Olivier quietly asked Pascal if he had noticed anyone lurking outside the gallery who might be their erotomaniac. Pascal had thought of it too and glanced outside a few times, but hadn't seen anyone. Olivier hadn't liked the police telling Amanda that sexual stalkers were very sly about remaining unobserved, and incredibly persistent. They said it wouldn't be unusual for him to pursue Amanda for six months to a year, or even two. Olivier didn't like the idea of that at all.

They were putting the finishing touches on the lighting when Olivier left. Amanda thought she would go home around eight or nine o'clock. Pascal was going to take her home, and she told Olivier she would be fine until he got there. He couldn't come until after Stephanie's birthday dinner, but he was planning to spend the night with Amanda. He didn't want her alone all night.

"I don't want you to miss out on time with your sons. I'll be safe on my own if you decide to stay at your place tonight. I'll just keep everything locked up."

"And if he climbs up the façade again, you'll be alone." She hadn't had time to have the window fixed yet.

"I'll have the alarm on. Seriously, don't worry about me." She was more frightened than she wanted to admit, but she didn't want to deprive him of the last hours with his boys. She was a small woman and a man could easily overpower her. But in any case, Olivier had no intention of allowing her to sleep in her apartment alone, until the erotomaniac had disappeared again, or the police caught him.

Olivier hurried off to change for dinner. He was taking Stephanie and the boys to Alain Ducasse for her birthday, and Elizabeth Bonnard always came with them, as part of Stephanie's birthday tradition. Stephanie wasn't quite as close to Veronique and Valerie, but Lizzie was like a younger sister to her. As part of their constant traveling to be in horse shows around the world, the four equestrian women actually spent more time with each other than with their families. It was true for Stephanie and Lizzie, and the birthday celebration wouldn't seem complete without her. Stephanie loved fine food, and Ducasse was one of her favorite chefs.

At dinner, the two young men talked about their plans. Edouard was going back to Geneva in the morning, having finished his internship at J.P. Morgan and been offered a permanent job. He loved working there and had learned a lot in the short time he'd been an intern. And Guillaume was flying back to Buenos Aires. He had a polo match in Uruguay in the coming week, in Punta del Este. He loved living in South America, and his Spanish was fluent now. Polo was a favored sport in Argentina, and he took it very seriously, just as his mother did her horses. He was good enough to be a professional but played on one of the best amateur teams.

"When are you leaving?" Olivier asked Stephanie casually, as they finished an excellent dinner.

"Why? Do you have plans?" she asked him with a pointed look, as Lizzie chatted easily with Edouard. They had grown up knowing her, she was almost like a young aunt to them, and they considered her a member of the family. She came from a good family of some stature in the Dordogne area in France, which was horse country. Her parents had excellent stables, and like Stephanie, she had grown up around horses. When Olivier asked her when she was leaving, Stephanie wondered if he would ever have the bad taste to bring a woman home with him when she was away. It was hard to imagine, but possible. Some of her friends' husbands had done similarly tasteless things while their wives were away. She thought Olivier was better than that, and more respectful, in spite of their long history of separate bedrooms and no sexual involvement.

"I just wondered if you're going to be in town. We are married, after all," he answered. He was going to Amanda's opening on Monday, and had no intention of telling Stephanie about it, or inviting her to go with him. They hadn't gone out socially together in about ten years.

"I have some things to take care of this week, and an appointment at the dentist. We need to be in England by next weekend, so I think we'll leave Thursday or Friday," she told him, and he nodded. "There's actually a small horse show sponsored by Hermès at the Grand Palais this week. They've been begging me to go as one of the judges. I haven't committed to it yet," she said vaguely.

The dinner ended on a warm note. They all went home in good spirits, dropping Lizzie off at her apartment on the way. The boys sat in the kitchen with their mother when they got home, and Olivier went to change into jeans and a sweater and joined them a few minutes later.

"You're going out?" his wife questioned him, surprised because of the late hour. He nodded and offered no explanation or information. He didn't want Amanda sleeping alone after the break-in.

"I'll say goodbye to the boys tonight, since they're both leaving so early in the morning." They were taking the earliest flights out of Charles de Gaulle Airport. Neither of their sons seemed to mind their father being absent for their departure at dawn. They thanked him for an excellent dinner and a good time. They had all been relaxed and in a good mood all evening. The birthday dinner had been a success, and Stephanie had enjoyed it. The boys went upstairs together to finish packing, chatting on the stairs to their rooms, and Stephanie looked at her husband with a quizzical expression.

"I take it you won't be home tonight," she said, and he was surprised by the question.

"Am I supposed to check in with you now?" he said, sounding testy. She hadn't asked him that in years, and he didn't feel he owed her an answer now. In any case, he wouldn't give it to her. "Why are you asking me that?"

"Just curious. You seem to be moving at high speed these days." More than ever before, as though he had an important destination to get to, which in his mind he did. He didn't want Amanda to be alone in her apartment overnight.

"You're not here nine months of the year, if not ten," he pointed out to her. "I don't think questions like that are in order." He liked the way it had been between them for the past twenty years, without explanations or the pretense that they should answer to each other. They had developed a philosophy of total freedom between them that he found easy to live with and that worked with his lifestyle. "We moved past that years ago."

She nodded agreement. What he said was true. "Sometimes I wonder if that was the right thing to do, for the children's sake. Maybe they needed parents as a unit, not just two separate individuals who love them. Do you ever think that?" She was curious about it.

"Never. We created a style that worked for us then, and still does, and the children adjusted to it, not the reverse. It's irrelevant now. They're grown up and gone," he reminded her. She had very old-fashioned ideas about childrearing that he didn't agree with. He and she were not of her parents' generation. Olivier always thought they should be more modern. And the boys hadn't seemed to suffer from having parents who weren't close and an absentee mother most of the time. And he'd been there, even if she wasn't.

"I just wondered what you thought. I feel guilty sometimes for how much I traveled when they were younger. They were still so little when I started going to all the big shows. You were a good sport to take care of them so I could do it. Thank you," she said kindly. It was the friendliest she'd been to him for a long time, and he wondered why. It seemed very late in the day to be warming up to him now, especially for him, with Amanda in the picture. "Don't worry, I'm not going to ask you to stay home and run the house while I'm away." There was nothing much to run now anyway. The kids were gone and so were they.

"That's good news, because I won't do it," he said easily.

"You seem very busy these days," she said, and sounded as though she was fishing.

"And so are you," Olivier reminded her. He didn't want a rapprochement, a "coming closer" with her now that he had met Amanda and was enjoying the freedom he'd had from Stephanie for years. He wondered if she sensed that he had someone important to him in his life and was shaken by it. If so, it would surprise him, but he knew that women had odd instincts about things like that. He and Stephanie had been strangers to each other for years, almost since the beginning. He had never understood her, and how incapable she had been of having a relationship with him. Their marriage had been a terrible mistake and he saw that Amanda was right about it. It had been an even bigger mistake to stay together. They should have moved on years ago. He was sure of that now.

With the children as their excuse, they had been lazy about starting new lives on their own, and making whatever financial sacrifices they would have had to. Having less money would have been better than twenty-six years of a loveless marriage. And it couldn't have been good for their kids either, although they had survived it. But what example had they had of a solid, loving relationship between a man and a woman? None at all. Their parents' relationship had been cold and distant, with one absentee parent.

He went to say a last goodbye to the boys after that, hugged each of them one more time, and left the house quietly. He drove to Amanda's apartment, thinking of her stalker and the break-in, and hoped there had been no further incident that night when she got home. She would have called him if there had been, and she hadn't.

It was late now, nearly midnight after their dinner out at Ducasse for his wife. He felt strangely liberated when he got to Amanda's house. He had done his duty with his wife and sons, and provided a nice birthday for her, and now he was following his heart to Amanda's front door, where he wanted to be that night, and where he felt he belonged now, and was so warmly welcomed. Stephanie had never been able to break through her own reserve to take him into her heart. Something had stopped her, which he never understood. She just didn't have it in her to be an affectionate person, even with their sons. Even though he knew she loved them, she always acted more like an aunt than their mother. They didn't seem to hold it against her. They accepted her as she was.

He rang the intercom to let Amanda know he was coming up and said it was him, and he used the door code he knew now. He bounded up the stairs, and found her standing in the doorway, with Lulu next to her. Smiling, she put her arms around his neck as he kissed her and carried her into the apartment, with Lulu barking and doing her welcome dance. Olivier smiled at Amanda after he set her down and closed the door.

"No problems tonight?" he asked.

"None. All my underwear is accounted for." It was an awful thought, and he followed her to her bedroom and sat down on the bed, where she'd been reading and waiting for him. "How was dinner?"

"Very nice. Delicious food, and everyone enjoyed it. I did my part." He stretched out on the foot of her bed, admiring her. "I said goodbye to the boys before I left."

"Did she know you went out?" Amanda asked, curious about the strange relationship he and Stephanie had.

"Yes. I didn't make a secret of it. She said I look very busy. Maybe she senses something. But after all this time, neither of us would have a right to question or fault the other for leading their own life. I don't ask her questions either. It would be total hypocrisy, given the decisions we made, to stick with it but lead separate lives. She has an uncanny instinct, though, for sensing when there's someone in my life, and that hasn't happened in quite a while."

"Do you think it bothers her?" Amanda asked softly, stretching her legs to where he was lying, as he gently massaged her foot. Everything about her was sensual and aroused him.

"I actually don't," he said in answer to her question. "She may be curious, but we never had the kind of relationship you and I do, and she wouldn't want it. I think she'd be horrified if I expected or demanded a real marriage from her. But she probably wonders if there's someone serious, and if it's a threat to the status quo that works so well for her. Divorce was always out of the question, but so was a real marriage. Maybe she's afraid that I would ask for a divorce if I found someone important to me, which would upset the apple cart for her. Divorce means public failure to her, and humiliation. Our marriage is a disaster and always has been, but no one knows that. She'd rather have a secret failure than an honest admission of defeat, and I went along with it for my own reasons. It was convenient for me too. It's not entirely her fault."

They stayed up until two in the morning talking, and made love. There were no late-night calls from her erotomaniac. Everything was peaceful, which was a relief, and they slept late the next morning. Olivier knew his boys were in the air by then, Edouard on his way to Geneva and Guillaume to Buenos Aires. He had no idea what

Stephanie's plans were and assumed she was with her horses at the stables, taking care of them, with her friends.

He and Amanda spent a lazy day, in her apartment, watching old movies. It had been a busy, stressful week, and she had another busy week coming, with the opening of the show the next day. He was planning to be there and was excited for her. It was a beautiful show. She said that she had some other plans that week. And he had some important meetings at work.

He left her around ten o'clock that night, after they had a late dinner, and she promised to turn on the alarm and call him if she had any problems. He had early meetings the next day, and it was easier to leave from his place, but he was slightly uneasy about leaving her.

He didn't see Stephanie when he got home, and her car wasn't in the garage. She was probably out with her friends.

He called Amanda when he got into bed, and they chatted for half an hour. She was asleep almost as soon as she set her phone down in the charger. She had a busy day ahead. And Olivier was smiling as he drifted off to sleep. He was planning to be back in Amanda's bed the next night, and hopefully forever, if all went well in the coming months.

Chapter 10

Tom Quinlan stopped by to see Amanda at the gallery on Monday, to say hello and catch up. He said he was deep into the book, and happy with it. He glowed when he talked about it, and she told him about the break-in at her apartment, and he was horrified, and worried for her.

"Maybe you should hire some kind of night security to stand outside your building at night so no one can climb up the façade again, especially when you're asleep. That's dangerous, Amanda. You need to take it seriously. The guy could kill you or rape you if he gets in again."

"I know. I'm setting the alarm now at night. Hiring a security guard seems so extreme. I never realized that someone could climb up my building that easily, and I'm only on the second floor. The police say they see that all the time with old buildings, mostly for burglaries."

"You know, you can call me any time if you have a problem, or even if you're just scared. I work late when I'm writing, which is pretty much every day now. I'm happy to come over whenever you want or need me." She didn't tell Tom that Olivier was performing that function. She didn't want to ruffle his feathers. She just thanked him and let it go. And Pascal would have come too. Delphine, the artist he'd been so desperate to date, was seeing him regularly now. Knowing his reputation as a womanizer, she was keeping him on a short leash, and he didn't seem to mind. He had invited her to the opening that night. Amanda didn't mention the party to Tom. She suspected he'd get annoyed when Olivier was there, and she didn't want to deal with it. He was better as a lunch friend, one on one, in small doses, so he wouldn't get the wrong idea.

Amanda had a monstrously busy day, putting the final touches on the show. She double-checked everything with the caterer herself, spoke to the artist and told him how proud she was of his work. She rechecked the guest list, instructed their assistants, and rushed home to change. She wore a red dress, which matched the paintings and looked great on her. And she was back promptly twenty minutes before the first guests arrived.

The gallery was already full of people and noise and all the signs of a successful party, with waiters carrying trays of hors d'oeuvres and champagne, by the time Olivier arrived. He'd gotten stuck at the office and the party was well underway.

"This looks like a major hit," he said, as he kissed Amanda and admired her dress. "You look fantastic!"

"Thank you!" She pointed to all the red dots on the walls next to the paintings. "We've sold all the paintings except two of the smaller ones. All the others are sold, even the biggest one." Olivier took a glass of champagne from a waiter and followed her around while she introduced him to people she wanted him to meet. She was proud to be standing with him, a feeling she hadn't had for a long time, and Olivier hadn't either.

"Am I allowed to say you two make a very handsome couple," Pascal whispered to her, when he saw her in her office, getting out a bio of the artist for one of their clients. She didn't remind him that Olivier already was a couple, and didn't like to think about it herself, but it was the truth.

"I like your friend Delphine. She's on to you." Amanda laughed at him. "I think you've met your match." Pascal grinned happily and nodded.

"Some show, huh?" he commented, as they went back to rejoin the guests. "It's the best one we've had in three years. And I think we're going to sell the last two paintings before the night is over. But the artist is willing to do commissions. He's very pleased."

"Me too," Amanda echoed.

The guests stayed until nearly ten o'clock, and after that Pascal and Delphine and Olivier and Amanda took the artist and his wife to the Fontaine de Mars and had a delicious dinner to celebrate.

Olivier spent the night with Amanda, knowing they were both going to be busy for the next two days and wouldn't be together in the evenings until he came back to sleep. He had an author dinner one night and then a publishing event for writers and agents, and she was going to two big social events herself, for charity, one of which was an art auction she had contributed a small painting to.

* * *

The night after the gallery opening, Amanda went to a charity event, given by Hermès. It was an equestrian jumping competition they did every year, which was attended by all the city's socialites, celebrities, and trendsetters, with a very glamorous guest list. Amanda was handed a brochure when she arrived, and she was startled to see Mme. Olivier Saint Albin listed as one of the judges. Amanda was slightly shocked at first, and curious to see what Olivier's wife looked like. There was a photograph of her in the brochure on one of her horses, winning first prize. Amanda wondered if Olivier was there, but he had told her he was having dinner with an author he was encouraging to finish a book he was convinced would be a bestseller, and she believed him. She ran into a friend then, and got caught up in meeting people and introductions, and was introduced to a member of the Dumas family, which owned Hermès. She got swept up in their group then, and suddenly someone was introducing her to the judges of the event, since the equestrian part of the evening hadn't started yet. Amanda found herself shaking hands with a tall, serious, distinguished-looking woman wearing a black Chanel suit, her dark hair in a tight bun, and very little makeup, if any. She was a handsome woman, although not beautiful, and Amanda thought she had a gentle look in her eyes when she shook her hand and made small talk with her, fascinated that she was meeting Olivier's wife. Stephanie had no idea who she was.

Amanda couldn't resist asking her, "Is your husband here with you?" She felt like a total fraud inquiring, and Stephanie shook her head.

"No, he isn't. Do you know him?" She seemed surprised at that. People didn't usually ask her about Olivier. Many of her friends had never even met him.

"I think he came to an opening at my gallery once," Amanda said vaguely.

Stephanie nodded then, that made sense. "He's not a fan of equestrian events." She introduced Amanda then to a petite redheaded younger woman, in a short sexy black dress and high stiletto heels, with a pretty face, wearing bright red lipstick. Everything about the two women seemed opposite to an almost comic degree. They talked for a few more minutes, said that they were riding partners on the same circuit, and were leaving for a show in England the next day. The redhead disappeared into the crowd with a glass of champagne, and Olivier's wife went to the dais and took her place with the other judges. A bell had sounded, and the event itself was about to start.

Amanda was shaken by having met Stephanie, who was nothing like what she had imagined. She had a schoolteacher look to her and was surprisingly plain in her severe black suit with her hair pulled back. She was the French equivalent of a Park Avenue matron. She'd been wearing flat black suede Hermès loafers and dark stockings, with a string of pearls around her neck. She was one of those women who looked like she was accustomed to wearing a uniform and had no idea what to wear when she wasn't. Her riding partner, on the other hand, had no trouble figuring it out at all, and was very pretty with her wild red hair and big blue eyes, and the very short sexy dress and high heels.

Stephanie looked very official and serious once she took her place on the dais and put on glasses. And a few minutes later, the jumping competition began. Amanda stayed for about half of it, and then slipped away, called an Uber, and left.

She thought about Stephanie all the way home. There was something subtly sad about her, as though she had been disappointed by life, and wasn't quite sure why it had turned out that way. She didn't look like a mean woman, or manipulative. If anything, Amanda felt sorry for her. She felt almost guilty stealing her husband from her. And they were such an odd match.

Maybe when they had married, in their early twenties, youth and innocence had masked who they would turn out to be later, but who they were as adults was very different. Olivier was so vital and alive and exuberant, so dashing, exciting, and handsome. There was a strong current within him, a kind of creative electricity Amanda found irresistible, and that had caught her attention from the beginning. Stephanie seemed painfully shy and uncomfortable, and austere. Amanda was sure she had much more self-assurance on horseback in the realm that was familiar to her, but she was socially awkward, which made her seem unfriendly, and even cold. Amanda suspected Stephanie probably wasn't as cold as she looked, she was just out of her element. Maybe that was why she wanted the protective covering provided by a husband, even in name only. Without that, she was on her own.

Amanda could see why they never went out together and had no shared social life. They were a striking mismatch in every way. Stephanie appeared to be all sharp edges and pointy corners, unlike Olivier, who was socially smooth and very charming. Amanda couldn't picture the two of them being friends, let alone married.

She and Olivier were a much better match than he and his wife were. Stephanie seemed defenseless somehow, and losing Olivier would strip her of the protection she thought she needed to face the world. Amanda felt wrong being part of their odd relationship. If Olivier wanted to leave his wife, it had to be his choice. Amanda didn't want to pull him out of it, leaving Stephanie bleeding on the side of the road. Amanda wasn't even sure he'd have the courage to leave Stephanie, now that she'd seen her and talked to her. She could see why he had stayed married to her and hadn't insisted on a divorce. Just staying in it was easier, and they each had their own life, with no common ground, doing what they wanted. She couldn't imagine living that way. But having met Stephanie, she didn't see how Olivier could divorce her, and she questioned if he would. She seemed vulnerable as much as awkward.

Amanda tossed and turned all night, thinking about it. And the icing on the cake was a series of calls at three in the morning that she didn't answer, but guessed was the breather. She was so annoyed by it she couldn't sleep afterward, and as a result she looked haggard in the morning when she got to work. Olivier had slept through the calls. He'd had a lot of wine to drink with the author he was mentoring.

"Ow, looks like you had a rough night. The stalker?" Pascal asked her. Olivier had rushed out to another early meeting, and she never had a chance to tell him she had met Stephanie the night before.

"Yes, at three A.M. But other stuff before that. I met Olivier's wife last night."

"On purpose?" Pascal's voice was a high-pitched squeak of astonishment when he asked her.

"No, by accident. I went to a charity equestrian event, sponsored by Hermès. She was one of the judges, she's a big horsewoman."

"Does Olivier know you met her? Was he there?"

"No. He wasn't there. He had an author dinner. I haven't told him yet, I didn't talk to him this morning. I think he was out late, drinking heavily with the author. I was asleep when he came home."

"He probably won't like that you met her."

"He'll never divorce her," she said, looking glum.

"Why not? Is she pretty?" Amanda shook her head, feeling mean when she did.

"No, at first glance she looks stern, like a schoolteacher. She's very awkward, plain-looking, and kind of sad. They were childhood friends and got married right out of university. She's nothing like him. She's tall, but sort of mousy, like a very big mouse. There's no fight in her, no spirit, no bright light within. I don't see how he'll divorce her, and then I'm the one who'll get hurt, because he'll think I'm strong enough to take it and she isn't. That's what happened to me last time. I don't know, Pascal. I think I'm the one heading for a fall, and they'll stay married. She's not the kind of woman you divorce. She's very uptight and proper, and I think he doesn't want to hurt her, or get hurt himself."

"You don't know that. Talk to him about it." She nodded and went to her office, but she was depressed all day thinking about it.

She didn't see Olivier until late that night, when he came to spend the night with her after the publishing event. He was happy to see her after two days of being too busy to talk to her. They sat in her study and chatted, and he had the feeling that something was bothering her, but she didn't say what at first. It wasn't until they went to get ready for bed that she looked at him in the mirror after brushing her teeth, still holding her toothbrush.

"I met your wife yesterday," she said quietly.

"You what?" He was stunned, and for a moment thought Amanda had gone to see her.

"I met Stephanie," she repeated.

"How? Did you call her?" He looked shocked.

"Of course not. I would never do that. I went to the Hermès equestrian event and someone introduced me to her. She was one of the judges."

He was calmer then. "I think she said something about it a few days ago. I wasn't paying attention. How did she look?"

"Uncomfortable," Amanda said, and he smiled.

"She probably was. She hates big social events, or even small ones."

"She was very proper and distinguished, different than I expected. She doesn't match you somehow. I can't envision you with her, even as a kid." Stephanie looked dead to Amanda, but she didn't say that to Olivier. She seemed like she had given up on life.

"I assume you didn't mention the connection between us," he said cautiously.

"Of course not. But I can't see how you're going to divorce her. She seems like an unhappy person. That's hard to walk away from without being crushed by guilt."

"I don't feel guilty. I didn't do anything wrong, most of the time, or not that she knows of," he corrected himself.

"She'll blame you in the end, and me. And your kids will hate me when they see how sad their mother is."

"She's always sad. She isn't predisposed for happiness, or even to give it. Except if it's something to do with horses or her friends. She's happy with them, not with me."

"Olivier, you're never going to divorce that woman," Amanda said, certain of it. She was cold but seemed fragile and disappointed by life.

"When the time is right, I could, I am, I will," he said in a tone of desperation. He could feel Amanda slipping away from him. She was afraid again, of his marital status and of getting hurt.

"I don't believe you. She looks helpless. You're too kind a person to do that to her. And maybe I am too. I don't want to be the adulteress, the mistress, the bad guy. If you had paid me to tell her the other night, I couldn't have. She just looks beaten and sad and like life didn't turn out right for her, and she isn't sure why."

"All of that is true," he admitted. "But I have a right to a life too, and to happiness. She comes alive at her horse shows. You don't see that side of her. She's a different person there. She shines."

"No, I didn't see that," Amanda said quietly. "But what I'm afraid of seeing is me getting hurt, and you staying with her forever, leading the crazy life that you two invented because you didn't have the guts to divorce her. And she looks so respectable that I can see why you didn't. So you live this empty life and stay married to her. And I wind up brokenhearted again."

"We have to give it time. It won't happen overnight," or maybe ever, Amanda thought. "I told you I'd move out if you want me to. She's going away for a while now. I'll talk to her when she comes back. I don't want to do it over the phone. She'll be back in two months. Just give us enough time to find out how we get along, the two of us, and to find the best way to do this." And then Stephanie would be even sadder, and no matter what he did, it was going to be Amanda's fault, since she was behind it. Amanda could see it now.

"If you felt this way, you should have done it years ago."

"But I didn't. So now I have to figure out how, with the least amount of damage to everyone."

"I don't want to be the bad guy so you can clean up your mess. She doesn't deserve that, and neither do I," she said firmly. After they talked about it for a while longer, they argued, and finally went to bed and didn't make love. He went home the next morning, and found a note from Stephanie. There was a problem in England, so she had left earlier than planned. She was on the Eurostar as he read the note. She said she had a lot of prep work to do there for the shows. The note said she'd be in touch, but he knew she was away this time for two months. And now he had to wait two whole months to tell Stephanie he wanted out. He just hoped Amanda would wait that long. He was panicked again, and he knew Amanda would be too. He showered and dressed for the office an hour later, and dreaded telling Amanda the news that night, that Stephanie had left before he could talk to her.

Chapter 11

Olivier was in a meeting late that afternoon when he heard his phone vibrate three times. He glanced at it, hoping it was Amanda. They'd had a rough night talking about his marriage and his wife. Having met Stephanie, Amanda no longer believed that Olivier would divorce her in the end. He was sorry they had argued. He hadn't heard from her that morning, and he wasn't sure he was going to after the night before. He didn't want to lose her. He had never loved a woman more.

When he looked at the number on his phone, he saw that it wasn't Amanda. He couldn't leave the room. It was a delicate negotiation and he had to wait until it concluded, and then he went to check his messages. The call was from Lizzie. He called her back and he could tell she'd been crying.

"Are you okay?" he asked her.

"Steph came off. Badly. She was thrown." Her voice was shaking.

"By one of her horses?" That surprised him. Hers were impeccably trained and docile.

"No, she was trying a horse she was thinking of buying. He wasn't fully broken yet. The breeder warned her. She wanted to try him anyway. She's pretty badly banged up. She's in surgery now."

"What did she break?" he asked, feeling panic race up his spine. What if she broke her back and was paralyzed? It had happened to others. It could happen to her too, and maybe it had. And he could never leave her then.

"She broke her pelvis and her shoulder, and they can't do anything about either one, they can't set them. And her right arm and leg. They're putting a titanium plate in her leg, and a steel bar in her arm." It sounded bad to him, but at least she wasn't paralyzed. "She was very brave. They let me ride in the ambulance with her. We're in Sussex. She'll be in the hospital for a week or so. After that, we can bring her home. She'll have to convalesce for a few months. She may need another surgery on the arm. She's going to miss all the shows for the next few months."

"But she's alive, and she's not paralyzed, right?"

"Yes," Lizzie said in a small squeaky voice.

"Does she have a head injury?"

"No, her helmet stayed on. She was wearing a new one."

"Thank God," he said fervently. She would recover, but from the sound of it, it would take time. "I'll find nurses for her," Olivier said, his mind racing. She would need care, and close attention. He was her husband. He couldn't just walk away now.

"The girls and I can take care of her," Lizzie offered, and he knew it was well meant, but not practical or adequate, from the sound of the gravity of the accident.

"She'll need professionals."

"We can help at least. Do you want to talk to the surgeon when he finishes?"

"Yes." He jotted down the number and the doctor and surgeon's names.

"The doctor said it would take five or six hours, maybe longer. You can call him after that. It's been two hours now." It was four o'clock. She would still be in surgery that night.

"I'll try to come over tonight, I have some meetings I have to re-schedule. At worst, I'll be there tomorrow," he promised.

"We're with her. We won't leave her. They're going to put a cot in her room. We'll take turns spelling each other off. I'll stay with her for the first twenty-four hours." Lizzie gave Olivier the name of the hospital in East Sussex. "Can we stay at the house when you bring her back?" Lizzie asked him nervously, she sounded like a child. Olivier and Stephanie had a guest room and the boys' two empty rooms, so there was space for them, and Stephanie would probably like it, but it was going to be an invasion, and he wasn't sure he could stay with Amanda now that things were rocky between them. But he wanted to tell her about the accident. And he had been plan-ning to stay with her that night to protect her from her stalker.

"Let me know how she is when she comes out of surgery. I'll call the doctor, and arrange to get her some nurses, and of course you can stay at the house when she gets back. I'm sure she'd love that. Thank you, Lizzie. I appreciate the help." He was feeling flustered and overwhelmed. He felt sorry for Stephanie, but this was not going to help his case with Amanda if he had to nurse his wife for the next three or four months, or longer. The mechanics of taking care of someone so badly injured were going to be complicated. Stephanie was lucky she had three devoted friends who were available and willing to help. And Olivier was lucky to have them too, although he didn't entirely see it that way yet. It was more than he could manage with a daily housekeeper, a publishing house to run, and a girlfriend who was about to bolt out the door.

He left the office at five to go home and pack a bag to take to England, and afterward stopped at the gallery to see Amanda. She was busy with a client, and he waited and chatted with Pascal. Pascal saw immediately that something was wrong, but Olivier wanted to tell Amanda first. He had talked to the doctor by then. Stephanie was still in the operating theater with the surgeon. There had been some shattering of the bones she'd broken, and it took time to put her back together. The doctor thought she could travel in a week, better by car or even by ambulance than by plane or train, to get her back to Paris. And it would be bed rest and physical therapy after that. The doctor said her recovery could be anywhere from three to six months. Olivier felt as though he had been sucked back into his marriage just when he wanted to leave it and had promised Amanda he would. She didn't believe he'd do it, and this wasn't going to help convince her. And she was compassionate enough that she would expect him to take care of his wife. Stephanie would assume it too. An event like this was one of the few times, maybe the only one, when she'd expect him to act like a husband and needed him.

Amanda finally got free of her client and came looking for him.

Triangle

She had seen Olivier come in, and looked for him in Pascal's office. The two men were talking in subdued tones. He had told Pascal something had happened, and Pascal said he was sure that Amanda would understand. Olivier followed her into her office, looking serious. She could see that something was wrong. He was carrying a small heavy briefcase, with files he needed to work on, and an overnight bag. He still wanted to spend the night with her, if she'd have him, and then leave for England in the morning.

He sat down across from Amanda, on the far side of her desk. "Stephanie had an accident in England this morning," he said bluntly.

"Oh my God, is she all right?" He looked like he was going to tell her she was dead.

"She will be. It's painful but not life-threatening. Broken arm with a steel rod in it now, shattered leg, a steel plate, broken pelvis and shoulder. None of it will kill her, but she'll be in a lot of pain. The women she rides with are with her now. I'm going over tonight or tomorrow, and I'll bring her back. They're going to stay in the house with her when she comes home, which is incredibly nice of them, and she'll need nurses for a while."

"You have to be there too," she said sternly.

"Yes. I'll keep an eye on things. I'm not much of a nurse, and I have a company to run. I'll hire nurses for her. I'm not trying to shirk my responsibilities, Amanda. Stephanie's friends volunteered to stay. They want to. And she'll probably want that too. This doesn't change any of what I want to do, or how I feel about you. I probably can't broach the subject with her for a while, until she's better, but nothing's changed for me, and hopefully not for you."

"I don't know," she said softly, looking at him sadly. "I love you,

161

Olivier, but I don't have the feeling you'll divorce her. Maybe you're more married than you think. She's a decent woman. I could see that. She's not some bitch you want to escape, or you would have years ago."

He looked outraged at the suggestion. "That's not true. I owe her something now, obviously. Ever since I met you, I've known how wrong that marriage is, and how wrong I was to keep living a lie with her, so no one would be shocked or embarrassed or disapprove. Even if you leave me now, I'm still going to ask her for a divorce. It's long overdue. Will you give me the time I need to work this out? A little more time because of the accident, but not forever. I promise you, I will be a free man, and then it will be up to you if you want me or not." She smiled a small wintry smile at him, and wanted to believe him, but she wasn't sure she did.

"I think we both need to think about it," Amanda answered him, which was not the response he wanted. He wanted her to say that she loved him and she'd wait forever. But he wasn't going to take forever. He didn't want to. "Take care of your wife," Amanda said. "Bring her home, see how it's all working out, and we'll talk. You need to be very sure you want to do this, and if you really think you can. Maybe neither of you wants that in the end. Maybe what you have now is right for you. I can't judge that, and I shouldn't have pushed you. That's not fair. People make the compromises that work for them. It's worked for both of you for a long time. I have no right to interfere and steal you from her." It was a role she didn't want.

"You're not stealing anything from anyone," he tried to reassure her, but he could see she didn't believe him. Amanda was an honorable woman, and she didn't want to break up a marriage if it was viable. She thought it was, and Olivier swore it wasn't. She thought he and Stephanie were ill-suited, but there had been enough there for them to cling to it and keep it on life support for twenty-six years. Amanda didn't want to be the one to pull the plug on their marriage. That was up to him.

"Call me and let me know how it's going when you get back," she said sadly. "I hope she feels better soon."

"It'll take a while. Amanda, I love you, more than I can tell you or you can imagine. Please don't give up on us." There were tears in his eyes when he said it, and in hers.

"Can I spend the night with you tonight? I can go to England in the morning," he said softly, and she shook her head.

"You need to think about this. Go and see to your wife now. And Olivier, I love you too," she whispered, as the tears spilled onto her cheeks. He walked around her desk and took her in his arms and held her. She was shaking, and she walked him out after that. Pascal saw them go but he didn't say anything. They needed to be alone.

Olivier hailed a cab and left for the airport. He had to get to London and from there drive to East Sussex. Amanda walked back to her office, and was crying when Pascal came in to check on her a few minutes later.

"Are you okay?" he asked her, sitting down in the chair Olivier had just vacated.

"No," she said, and smiled through her tears. "Olivier's wife had a bad accident."

"That's rotten luck, for all three of you," Pascal said. "I didn't trust him when you first told me about him, but I do now. He just has to clean up his life. I know it's a big deal, but I think he'll do it, for you. He seems like a good man, and he loves you."

"He has to do it for him. And I'm not so sure he will. He'll have to take care of her for months. Maybe they'll rekindle their marriage. Maybe it was never as dead as he thought."

"I think King Tut has a better shot at another round than that marriage, from what Olivier's told me. It's been dead for decades. Some things can't be revived. He doesn't love her, he loves you."

"We'll see," she said, and blew her nose in her handkerchief.

Olivier was on his way to the airport by then, with a heavy heart, as much for him and Amanda as for Stephanie. At least she would be heavily sedated and feeling no pain for the next several weeks, but he and Amanda wouldn't be.

Pascal offered to stay with Amanda that night and she insisted she'd be fine alone and would turn on the alarm. She spent the night crying, with Lulu in her arms, remembering the nights she had spent with Olivier. She wanted to have the strength to give him up, before he destroyed her with promises he couldn't keep. And Olivier would have to take care of his wife.

Olivier took a nine P.M. flight to London and landed at Heathrow at nine-thirty local time. He gained an hour with the time difference. He rented a car and was on the road to Sussex by ten. He got there at one in the morning. He walked into Stephanie's hospital room. She was groggy and half asleep after the surgery, with tubes everywhere and a nurse in the room with her. Lizzie was there too, holding her hand. Stephanie recognized him when he stood next to her bed and patted her other hand.

"I told you horses are dangerous beasts. You never listen." Olivier smiled at her, and Lizzie smiled too. She was like a daughter or a sister to Stephanie.

"What are you doing here?" Stephanie asked him. She hadn't expected him to come. She had her friends with her. And Lizzie hadn't told her he was coming, in case he changed his mind, or something went wrong, or he couldn't leave his office in time to arrive that night.

"I thought I'd come to London for some theater, and kidney pie." He hated kidney pie, and she knew it. "I'm sorry you got hurt, Stephie." He hadn't called her that since they were kids.

"I don't think I'll buy that horse. He's a little frisky," she said sleepily, and he laughed.

"Yeah, I think that's about right. Frisky."

"When can I go home?" she asked him. The surgeon hadn't told her.

"I have to see your doctor. He thinks you should go by ambulance, and not mess with the plane or train."

"Can we hitch the horse trailers to it?" she asked him, and he laughed again.

"I think maybe we'll send the horses separately. I'm not sure the ambulance drivers will want to pull three triple horse trailers. The girls will take care of it, I'm sure." He patted her hand again. He didn't kiss her, but he was there. She knew he was a good man.

"Don't tell the boys I got hurt. They'll just worry. I'm fine. You didn't need to come," she said staunchly. She looked uncomfortable that he was there, and Lizzie didn't leave her side, there was a cot for her in the room.

"Yes, I did. For what it's worth, we're married and I'm your husband. This is what husbands do." There was very little of the role he still provided her, and they both knew it. And she was no wife to him either. But after twenty-six years of a failed marriage, at least they were friends.

"Thank you," she said softly. As he looked at her, he wondered if Amanda was right. He felt a responsibility for this woman, no matter how dead their marriage was. She was still his wife, and he had deep affection for her. He felt sorry for her. She was obviously in a lot of pain, and trying not to show it. A nurse came in then to check on her, and Olivier walked out to find her friends in a small waiting room, worried about her. They were her family more than he was.

"She looks better than I thought she would," he said to them in hushed tones. Lizzie joined them a few minutes later and said she was asleep. They were giving her morphine and would for the next few days.

"Where are you all staying?" Olivier asked them.

"Nowhere. We just got here," Valerie said. "We were going to London tonight after she saw the horse. Our horses went on to the stable outside London. The nurses said there's a hotel nearby. But we'd be fine here until the morning."

"I'll stay," Lizzie said immediately. She looked tired and worried, and her red hair was in a wild tangle. She hadn't combed it since that morning, and didn't care. She was concerned for her friend. They all were. They worked out a schedule then, taking turns sitting with her, and Olivier volunteered to take a shift. Lizzie said she didn't mind double shifts, but the others said she needed some sleep too. She hadn't left Stephanie since the accident.

Valerie and Veronique left with Olivier, and Lizzie stayed with Stephanie to sleep on the cot in her room. They agreed to regroup in the morning and start taking shifts with her, and then they took off to find the hotel. When they returned in the morning, the doctor told Olivier that Stephanie could go home in four or five days if there were no complications, and there didn't seem to be. Olivier and the three women fell into a routine. They all stayed at the same small, simple inn nearby, and Olivier paid for all their rooms. And Veronique called the stable outside London to check on their horses. They had three grooms with them, who would drive the trailers back to Paris. The three women had two horses each, and Stephanie had three. Nine horses in all, in three triple trailers. They decided to send them back immediately. There was no point keeping them in England. None of them would be riding in the shows now. And Stephanie wanted to go home. The doctor thought it would be safe for her to travel by ambulance in a few days, and her three friends would stay at the house with her, along with two nurses Olivier hired through their doctor in Paris. Stephanie was being very brave and was eager to leave.

Olivier called Amanda every day from England, two and three times a day. She had cried since he left, sure that the accident would ultimately end their affair.

"How is she?" she asked him.

"Better than she could be in the circumstances, very lucky in fact.

She's in a lot of pain, but she's tough and very strong. Her friends have been staunch and terrific. If I ever have an accident, I hope someone calls them. Horse people stick together, and they've been friends for a long time. They don't really need me, but I thought I should be here. I feel sorry for Stephanie, she must hurt like hell. Or she will when the drugs wear off."

"It sounds awful," Amanda commiserated. "And how are you? Holding up?"

"I feel a little out of place, she was surprised to see me, as if I don't belong here, but it was the right thing to do to come," he said with a sigh. But he missed Amanda terribly, and hated the fact that she wasn't sure of them anymore. He wanted to reassure her and didn't know how. And Stephanie was in no condition for him to broach the subject of a divorce with her now, and she wouldn't be for a while. And every day he waited, Amanda drifted further away. He could hear it in her voice.

Getting Stephanie back to Paris four days later was a major event. Olivier hired a nurse for her, and a private ambulance, and getting her settled comfortably took all four of her entourage and the nurse to get her in the right position. The horses had already gone back to Paris, and were fine. Stephanie kept asking about them. She had pain medications for the drive, and Lizzie sat on a little seat next to her and held her hand. Olivier drove Valerie and Veronique in a rented car he could return in Paris. They followed the ambulance, and it took six hours to get back to Paris. They bought sandwiches at roadside food stores so they could keep driving, and after the first hour, with a morphine shot the nurse gave her, Stephanie slept the rest of the way. Olivier had hired nurses for her in Paris, to take care of her round the clock, although Stephanie's riding friends were disappointed not to be her only caretakers. It was chaos at first with so many people underfoot: the three women friends, the four nurses, and the patient. Olivier was going to be living with a total of eight women, at least five of them present at all times, and he was going to take a shift with her every day to relieve the others.

The ambulance drivers brought Stephanie upstairs to her room on a gurney, and the nurses had rented a hospital bed with Olivier's permission. Putting her to bed was painful for her, but she was happy to be home. She smiled once she was in the hospital bed in her room.

"The only thing missing are your horses in the garden so you could see them from your window," he said to her. Stephanie smiled at him, grateful for all he had done. And having her three friends around her made it seem like a party. Olivier fled to his office with relief. It had been a rugged week for them all.

He called Amanda as soon as he got to his office, to see how she was. She sounded sad but said she was fine. He invited her to lunch, but she turned him down. In her mind, he was back in the fold with his wife, and would most likely stay there, which wasn't how he viewed it at all. She was trying to protect herself. And all he wanted was to see her as soon as he returned.

"How is she?" she asked him politely.

"It was complicated getting her home. And I feel like I'm living in a women's dormitory. That's a lot of females under one roof."

"The little redhead looks like fun," she commented. Lizzie was roughly the same age as Amanda, but much more outspoken and still something of a tomboy at thirty-eight. But she was gently attentive to Stephanie and all her needs.

Once he was with them in the aftermath of the accident, Olivier realized how close they all were and how attached to each other. Stephanie had replaced her family and her husband with the three women. It startled him at times, but they were respectful of him and completely dedicated to her. One of them sat in her room at night, and the nurse sat in the hall. They called her into Stephanie's room when they needed to move her, or for the bedpan she had to use, or for more pain medication. With the broken pelvis and damaged leg, she couldn't stand or put any weight on that side. And crutches were impossible with the broken shoulder and arm. All she could do was lie in bed, watch TV, sleep, eat, and talk. She was still too drugged on the pain meds to read, or to stay awake for long.

Olivier stopped in to visit her for a few minutes from time to time, and saw her when he took his shift, but he wasn't a constant presence the way her women friends were, and they were clearly the company she preferred. She panicked if one of them wasn't in the room with her. And Lizzie almost never left her side.

Amanda turned down Olivier's repeated invitations to lunch, and didn't want to see him. She said that both of them needed to think, and to see what happened with Stephanie when she recovered. She was convinced the accident would bring them back together and heal their marriage, and she didn't want to tempt Olivier or interfere. He stayed out of the house as much as possible. He had dinner with Pascal one night as a way to get closer to Amanda. Olivier explained the situation to him, and Pascal thought Amanda would calm down. He had become Olivier's staunch supporter.

"She doesn't want to be responsible for breaking up your marriage, and she thinks you'll stay with your wife now. She's been through that before, and it took her a long time to get over it," Pascal explained.

"That's not going to happen here," Olivier insisted, but his assurances were falling on deaf ears with Amanda. Pascal was more inclined to believe him. Amanda wouldn't let Olivier near her. She was afraid she'd melt and lose her resolve if she saw him.

The weeks were painful for Olivier as he watched Stephanie recover slowly. She was still the same woman who had never been the right match for him, or he for her, from the beginning. He felt sorry for her, but her accident didn't bring them any closer. It was obvious that she preferred the company of her friends. It didn't upset him, he was happy for her. At least she had friends she enjoyed being with. Watching them together, Olivier envied her. She had created an alternate world for herself. He was pining for Amanda and there was no one else he wanted to talk to. There was no question in his mind, Amanda was the love of his life. All he could do now was pray and hope she came to the same conclusion. There was no sign of it for now.

Chapter 12

Pascal repeatedly tried to get Amanda to see Olivier, even for a walk, a cup of coffee, a glass of wine, a meal, something, but her refusals were constant. She was trying to get over him and convinced she was doing the right thing, for both of them and for his wife.

"He says he's not going to stay with his wife when this is over. He'll move out. He sounds definite about it," Pascal assured her. "I believe him."

"That's what he says now. He's running a nursing home for her. He wouldn't do that if he didn't love her. He probably doesn't realize he does. He'll figure it out when the crisis is over. He wouldn't have stayed married to her for twenty-six years if he didn't."

"Some people are just stubborn. He's an honorable, decent guy. He's trying to do the right thing. That doesn't mean he wants to stay married to her."

"I think it does," Amanda insisted. "I was blinded by his charm. I should have known better. It's not right. I'm not going to get in the way of his marriage."

"He says his relationship with her is dead."

"So is ours," she said firmly. Pascal didn't believe her.

He noticed that she wasn't accepting any social invitations. She was mourning Olivier, and spending quiet evenings at home with Lulu, insisting the little dog was enough company for her for now and all she wanted. What she really wanted was Olivier, but he was married. Amanda had made a decision not to continue their relationship and was sticking by it, no matter how painful it was for her. She thought she was doing the right thing, whatever it cost her.

Tom called Amanda to tell her he had almost finished the book. He only had a few more chapters to write and was enjoying the warm late spring weather in Paris. He invited her to lunch, and she was going to turn him down, but on the spur of the moment, she decided not to. She hadn't been anywhere in weeks, and it was a beautiful sunny day, flowers were in bloom, the trees were blossoming. In a way, the abundance of nature made her even sadder. She would have liked to be sharing it with Olivier, but had decided that that was not her destiny. Nor was Tom, but lunch on the terrace of the Grand Palais sounded appealing. He was loving all the Paris museums, whenever he took a break from the book.

She met him at the restaurant on a slow day at the gallery, and Pascal said he'd cover for her. His own romance with Delphine was going well, and he was seriously smitten with the young artist. She was proving to be a match for him, as Amanda had said.

"So, did you figure out the ending of the book?" she asked Tom after they ordered lunch, and he looked pleased when he answered.

"Yes, I did."

"How does it end?"

"He kills her." She was surprised. The heroine was the main love interest throughout the book, and he'd been in love with the character since the beginning.

"That's a little harsh, isn't it?"

"Not really. He loves her so much, he can't bear to think of their love affair ever ending and someone else having her, so he kills her." It was definitely a dark twist to the plot.

"And then what? He goes to prison, or he gets away with it, or you leave the reader hanging?"

"He gets away with it. They never figure out who did it."

"Well, it sounds exciting. How are you doing finding an agent?"

"I found one in New York I like. I'm going to send him the manuscript as soon as I finish it. I told him about the ending, and he likes it. He said there's a market for that kind of dark book."

"Well, that's good." Amanda didn't want to discourage him. She generally didn't like thrillers anyway. They made her anxious.

"What about you? Still seeing Olivier the Magnificent?"

She was amused by the name and shook her head. "No, not really."

"A big nasty breakup?"

"No, his ex-wife had a terrible accident, and he's taking care of her. It seemed like a good time to make my exit." Tom nodded, looking pensive. She didn't want him to know that Olivier was still married. It was none of his business.

"I think I might use that. She has an accident. He nurses her tenderly. And *then* he kills her, so he's sure she knows he loves her before he does."

"That sounds a little complicated. I won't suggest it to Olivier," she said, as their lunch arrived. She had lost weight, as trying to get over Olivier had taken a toll. Tom had commented that she looked thinner. He did too, and his hair was longer. He was wearing jeans instead of khakis, and he looked a little less like an American college boy. It always struck her that his appearance and style really hadn't changed in twenty years, since they'd dated. But he seemed just a bit more European than he had when he arrived. And he had accomplished what he had come to do, write his book. "So, what are you going to do when you finish the last chapters?" she asked him.

"Get drunk and celebrate," he said with a boyish grin. "And travel around Italy for a while. Italy, Spain, maybe Copenhagen and Prague, Vienna, Venice."

"That sounds fun." Amanda smiled at him. It had seemed so odd to her when he had surfaced, around the same time Olivier did, but now it just seemed like a moment of nostalgia from their youth. And he seemed to have gotten over his romantic illusions about her. She just wanted to be friends, and he appeared to have understood. He told her about a movie he'd seen and loved, and she said she hadn't seen it. She hadn't been in the mood to do anything since Olivier had become Stephanie's head nurse and she'd stopped seeing him. But she was starting to get used to his absence, and trying to be philosophical about it, but she was still sad and she missed him. "When are you going back to L.A.?"

"I'm not sure. I think I'll travel all summer, and figure it out in September. I'm in no hurry to go back. I want to see if I can sell the book. That might be a whole new career for me. The law gets tedious at times."

Triangle

"That's impressive." Talking to him, she realized that she felt older than he was. His youthful appearance made him seem years younger to her.

"Do you want to see the movie with me? I think you'd love it. I wouldn't mind seeing it again. It's beautifully written, and the photography is incredible."

"Maybe I should," she said, thinking about it. "I haven't been out much recently."

"What about tomorrow? I'm going to start writing again this weekend." He was very disciplined about his writing. He had been that way in college too. And in law school. His magna cum laude was well deserved.

"Why not? I have nothing else to do, if it's as good as you say."

"It is." Even though she wasn't interested in a romance with him, it was nice having a friend to do things with. She had always enjoyed her male friends. Pascal had been her movie buddy, but ever since he got involved with Delphine, he had no time to do things with Amanda. Tom was perfect for that, and it sounded as though he'd be leaving soon to travel.

"I'll meet you at the theater," she suggested, as they left the restaurant. It had been a perfect lunch on a sunny day.

"I can pick you up," he offered. "I bought a beaten-up old Fiat. My chariot."

"Okay." She thanked him for lunch, kissed him on the cheek, and walked back to the gallery in the sunshine.

"How was lunch?" Pascal asked her when she got back.

"Nice." She smiled for the first time in ages. "We can actually be friends. He finally got the message."

177

"I'm glad. I'm sorry I've been so busy lately."

"I'm going to a movie with him tomorrow. It's some Hungarian movie he says is fabulous."

"It already sounds awful," Pascal said, laughing. "Enjoy it. You're not interested in him again?"

"Definitely not. I'm not ready for that yet anyway. I'm still nursing my broken heart," she said with a wistful smile that made Pascal's heart ache for her. Married men were just never a good idea, no matter how unmarried they said they were. They were never as free as they claimed. She'd learned that lesson now for good, the hard way.

Amanda was ready when Tom came to pick her up at her place the following evening after work. She was wearing jeans, a crisp white shirt, a pink sweater over her shoulders, and pink espadrilles. She looked almost as collegiate as he did. He was wearing jeans, a T-shirt, an old varsity jacket from Stanford in the school colors, and high-top Converse. The Fiat 500 he was driving was as beaten-up as he'd said. It made her feel young again. Her college boyfriend, a tiny battered student car, and going to a movie.

They bought popcorn at the theater, and she didn't love the movie as much as he did, though she could see why he would. The cinematography was excellent, but the storyline was a little too intellectual and seemed more like hard work. But it was nice to be out with a friend, doing simple things.

"Are you hungry? Do you want dinner?" he asked her as they left the theater.

"I had too much popcorn," she said. "I couldn't eat a thing."

Triangle

"Yeah, me too," he agreed. "Home?"

She nodded with a smile, and he headed toward her apartment. It had been a pleasant evening even if the movie wasn't great. It didn't really matter. She was coming back to the surface slowly, after Olivier. It was a hard recovery for her.

Tom parked his tiny car, and she turned to thank him before she got out, and before she could say a word, he grabbed her, kissed her hard on the mouth, and squeezed her breast. She was so startled she didn't know what to say for a minute, and he had been rough. Her breast still hurt.

"Tom, what are you doing? . . . Don't! No!" she said clearly, and she saw a look of fury in his eyes.

"Why not? Isn't that what you did with that pompous asshole you were so crazy about?" She opened the door to make a fast exit and he grabbed her again and pulled her back. He used both hands this time and tore her shirt open, ripping off all the buttons and grabbing both her breasts. He plunged his mouth onto hers and bit her lip, and then slid one hand from her breast to her crotch and grabbed it hard. "Come on, Amanda, I remember that virgin game you used to play. You were hot! And you still are. Are you still pining for that jerk? I bet you didn't play the virgin game with him. You were the hot little French girl with me then. Let's go upstairs and play that again." He looked like a madman as he leered at her, and she yanked herself backward, leapt out of his car, ran to the door of her building, and punched in the code. She shoved her way through it and slammed it, just as he got to the door and kicked it hard. He was shouting at her as he tried to force the door open and couldn't. He was yelling "Bitch!" as she ran up the stairs and let herself into her apartment, turning off the alarm and setting it again. She was shaking violently and felt like she was going to faint. He was insane. She had never seen that side of him before. It was a jealous rage, a thousand times more violent than he'd been in college. She had been sure for a minute that he was going to rape her. The front of her blouse was torn, the buttons had flown off, her bra was exposed, and she could still remember his grabbing her crotch after he brutalized her breasts. And she had thought they could be friends.

It took her an hour to calm down and stop shaking. He had yelled "You bitch" at her windows from the street and had driven away. He seemed dangerous to her. She was just grateful that she could get out of his car, and that he hadn't overpowered her. Did he really think that violence was going to work? He had looked like a madman while he mauled her. No one had ever done that to her before. In the end it wasn't just frightening, it was depressing that he thought he could treat her that way. And he clearly hated Olivier too, and was wildly jealous of him.

She lay awake for hours that night, clutching Lulu, and she had a bruise on each breast the next day. She was still looking pale and shaken when she got to the gallery and told Pascal about it, and he was horrified.

"So much for old college friendships," he said, outraged. She nodded, and something else had occurred to her during the night, which was even more frightening if it was true.

"I know this sounds crazy. But do you think he could have been the erotomaniac who climbed the wall to my apartment, broke in, and stole my things?" It sounded far-fetched when she said it, even to her, and Pascal shook his head.

"It does sound crazy," he confirmed. "The guy has some impressive degrees. He's smart, educated, went to one of the best colleges in the States, he's an attorney. He may be a pig the way he treats women, but a guy like that is not going to climb up a building, and risk killing himself, to steal your underwear. He could have come for a drink and stolen it while he used your bathroom. He's not a cat burglar or a pervert, he's just a shit," Pascal said with utter contempt. "If I ever see him again, I'm going to kick his ass," he said with a look of fury. "Do you want to call the police and file a complaint?"

"No, I don't. I never want to see him again. And what's the point of filing a complaint? They won't do anything to him. You're right, he wouldn't climb up the building for my underwear, he attacked me right there on the ground. Thank God I got into the building faster than he could. I think he might have raped me," she said seriously.

"Be careful coming in and out of your building for a while. Be sure he's not hanging around. And if he shows up here, I will call the police. I don't care if he is a lawyer. He's an asshole of the worst sort."

"He left bruises on my breasts," she admitted to him.

"That's awful. Do you want me to take pictures of them?" he offered. "Or one of the women can do it. Sorry, I didn't mean to sound like a voyeur. I hate the guy for doing that to you."

"Yeah. Me too. I don't want pictures taken. I'm not going to press charges. I just want to forget him. This isn't my year. A married man, a stalker, and a would-be rapist, all within a few months. I think I'll forget about dating for a while, even old friends. And the movie sucked, by the way," she said with a rueful grin.

"Just keep an eye out for him, and make sure he's not lurking around when you leave the gallery or go home at night. He probably won't bother you again, the rejection is too humiliating. But I do think there's something wrong with him to go around treating women that way." Pascal gave Amanda a hug and she got to work at her desk, but it had been a horrible night and a terrifying scene she knew she would never forget.

It took Amanda several days to calm down after Tom Quinlan's violent attack on her, and she had nightmares about him a few times. She told Pascal about it, and he said he didn't blame her. He took her out to dinner one night just to help her forget it and relax. He made fun of her because she brought Lulu with her. She had been taking her everywhere as her "emotional support dog," but she was so cute everyone loved her.

Pascal drove Amanda home that night after dinner, not letting her take an Uber. He wanted to be sure she got home safely. It was the first time she had gone out to dinner since Tom manhandled her, and she still seemed a little skittish and on edge.

He walked Amanda to her apartment door, and she opened it, turned off the alarm, and turned on the lights, and when she did, she gasped. Her apartment had been broken into again, only this time, it had been vandalized. Her white mohair couch had been slashed with a knife, and three of the paintings. They weren't her best ones, but they were valuable and she loved them. Her father's Picasso hadn't been touched, fortunately. She and Pascal walked into her bedroom together, and the canopy over her bed had been slashed to shreds, and over the painting of a ballerina who looked like her, the vandal had written "Bitch" in black marker in big letters. She started to cry when she saw what had been done. Pascal called the police for her. She didn't call Olivier this time. She wasn't his problem now, nor was he her protector and savior, or even her friend.

"Do you still think it wasn't Tom?" she asked Pascal while they waited for the police.

"I don't know," he said honestly. "Who would do something like this? A lunatic. A savage. He's neither one. He's an educated person." But the word "Bitch" certainly led one to wonder.

The vandal had used the same method of entry, scaling the building again and coming in through the bedroom window, despite the new security device she'd installed. He disabled it and came right over it, through the window.

The police took it seriously when they saw the damage. She had insurance for the paintings and the couch, but the wickedness of the destruction and the sheer violence of it was alarming. The officers took photographs, and she raised the question about Tom, described the incident in the car, and gave them his name and address.

Amanda and Lulu stayed at Pascal's that night, and he helped her clean up the mess in her apartment the next day and called the insurance adjuster for her.

She picked three new paintings at the gallery to hang in the place of the ruined ones. And she was sad about the beautiful Italian couch too. Whoever had done this was a madman, whether Tom or a stranger.

The police reported to her at the gallery the next day that they had interviewed Mr. Quinlan, and he had been very calm and polite and sympathetic. He was very sorry to hear about the incident, and gave them his card from the law firm. They assured her that they had no reason to suspect him, and he denied ever manhandling her. He said they had been lovers in college and recently renewed their romantic relationship. It hadn't worked out and she was angry at him, so he said she had cooked up the story against him, and it was all a lie. He discreetly suggested that she might even have done the damage herself for the insurance money. The police withdrew immediately after that and did not fingerprint him. It was her word against his, and his had been more convincing.

She was in tears at the humiliation when the police left the gallery. Pascal found it hard to believe that the officers were so gullible.

"Do you believe me?" she asked Pascal, and he walked over and hugged her.

"Of course I do. The guy is a practiced liar, and maybe he didn't vandalize your apartment, although I think he could have, but I fully believe that he tried to rape you. There's a screw loose in there somewhere. And the police officer who interviewed him just isn't as smart as he is. I want you to be even more careful now going out, or I'm going to get you a bodyguard. I'm beginning to think you need one, at least until your stalker is found. Somebody is committing these attacks on you. We have to find out who, and protect you in the meantime."

Amanda was just grateful she hadn't left Lulu in the apartment, because with a slash of his knife he might have killed her. Lulu was the only thing she cared about now. Paintings and a couch could always be replaced. Lulu couldn't.

* * *

Amanda went back to her office after the police left, to try to get some work done. And Pascal did something he normally wouldn't have done. He never meddled in other people's relationships. He figured it wasn't his business. But this time, he felt that Olivier deserved to know what was happening to Amanda. The attempted rape by Tom Quinlan, the second break-in, the destruction of her property and invasion of her home, and the fact that she was still pining for him. There was nothing Olivier could do about it either, but Pascal thought he should be aware of what she was going through and that she still loved him. And she needed safety and protection more than ever.

Olivier promised Pascal that he wouldn't tell Amanda he'd called, and when he hung up, he had tears in his eyes thinking of her. She clearly didn't want his help, or she would have called him. Instead, she was facing it alone. He sat for a long time with his head in his hands, trying to figure out how to help her and what to do next. He had some ideas, but she wouldn't take his calls. And he felt sick when he thought of Tom and what he had tried to do. Amanda didn't deserve any of what was happening to her, and he was powerless to stop it. In her eyes, he was just another married man, and she wanted nothing more to do with him. It made his heart ache, knowing how alone she must feel, and how frightened. He had asked Pascal to do all he could to help her and Pascal had assured him he would. Olivier was grateful he had called, and Pascal could hear that Olivier was on the verge of tears when he hung up. He felt terrible for both of them. Amanda was frightened and alone. And Olivier was powerless to help her. Amanda wouldn't let him.

Chapter 13

The weeks after Stephanie's accident had begun to seem interminable to Olivier. Her recovery was slow, and the army of people caring for her was constantly underfoot. The nurses were very professional and took good care of her. They needed help occasionally to move her and there was always someone around. The casts on her leg and arm were cumbersome, her shoulder was still painful, and the broken pelvis made it agony for her to sit. She was only comfortable when she was lying down, and even then she needed painkillers to get through the days and nights. Two physical therapists came, morning and evening. And Stephanie's three best friends were still staying in the house and always near at hand. They had canceled their summer plans and were tireless in their efforts to cheer her up. They took turns doing the cooking, which made it easier for Olivier since they had to feed the nurses too. There were always people around washing or feeding Stephanie, reading to her or changing her sheets. There was a constant babble of conversation. There were female voices everywhere. He was living with four women and a stream of daily workers. He lay down on his bed sometimes just to get a moment of peace. And it had been a particularly hot summer so far, which made it all seem more oppressive, particularly for Stephanie in her two casts.

She was enjoying the attention, and at times Olivier seemed over-whelmed. At the same time, he had to run his business, and their sons called him frequently for reports on their mother's condition. He felt like he was running a hospital, and he was seeing more of Stephanie than he had for twenty years. He saw her, but they never talked. And they were never alone, which he thought was just as well. He felt sorry for the pain she was in, but they had nothing to say to each other. They never had. Only his assistant at the office seemed to understand how stressed and tired he was. He covered it well the rest of the time.

The "Valeries," as he called them, since they were always together, were polite and solicitous whenever he saw them. They were grate-ful to Olivier for letting them stay with Stephanie. They were doing most of the cooking, and did it well. They had hired additional peo-ple at the stables to exercise their horses, and their whole focus was on their friend. And they thanked Olivier repeatedly for letting them stay at the house. They kept vases of flowers everywhere, and when-ever he came home, there were cooking smells in the air. He was sure that if they hadn't been there, Stephanie would have been seri-ously depressed. Of the three, Lizzie seemed to be the most devoted to her, alternately adopting the roles of sister, mother, daughter, and wife, and keeping her spirits buoyed. She massaged the limbs that weren't broken and read to her for hours sometimes until she fell asleep, and she kept the nurses on their toes, turning her when needed so she didn't get bedsores, and assisting the physical therapists.

Stephanie was determined to make a full recovery, and intended to be back on her horses as soon as she could walk and back on the show circuit soon after. She hated being an invalid and dependent on everyone around her, but they all contributed to make the process as painless as possible for her. And Olivier was well aware of how much time and energy it took. He was grateful they were there. He could never have done it himself without them.

He came into the room to bring Stephanie her mail one morning, having already eliminated all the bills, which he always paid. Stephanie contributed a small amount of her own money for the upkeep of her horses, which was considerable. Olivier had always paid the rest without complaint. It seemed a small price to pay to keep her happy, and on the road for most of the year with her friends. The marriage might not have survived if she had been home all the time with nothing to do. Supporting her life on the show circuit was a way of allowing them to have separate lives, which had been vital to both of them. Stephanie was missing that now, and so was he.

"How's our star patient today?" Olivier asked her cheerfully when he came into the room, with a stack of cards sent to her by a variety of people he didn't know. Their sons called her once a week. Her recovery was slow, but they knew she was in good hands, with their father and her friends.

"Tired of being flat on my back, and bored out of my mind. I miss my horses," Stephanie said plaintively.

"I'm sure you do." He had opened the cards for her since she couldn't do it with one hand. If he hadn't, the others would have done it for her.

"Are we driving you crazy? You're living with a whole army of women," she said sympathetically. "Is the house a mess?" She hadn't left the room in over a month. It was too hard, and painful for her, to move her.

"They're keeping it neater than you and I do." Olivier had nothing but praise for them. "I can see why some cultures encourage having several wives. I feel like I have four at the moment," he said, and she smiled.

"I'm sure you'll be happy when we all get out of your hair. Don't feel you have to be around all the time," she said. She had noticed that he was home a lot, and every night. "The girls can entertain themselves, and we're used to being on the road together." She hesitated, and watched him looking out the window in an unguarded moment. He seemed sad. He was thinking of Amanda and how long it had been since he'd seen her. It felt like an eternity to him, and he had nothing to look forward to now. At least Stephanie had her horse shows to go back to. In his mind, he had nothing without Amanda.

"You don't look happy," Stephanie said gently. "I thought you did for a while, and I figured you had someone new in your life. You always have a special spark and energy when you do. I hope I didn't screw that up for you with the accident." It was the most honest thing she'd ever said to him, and he was surprised. They were always guarded with each other, and he realized more than ever how little they knew of each other's lives, and even of who they were. "Did something go wrong?" Stephanie asked him, and for an instant, he was tempted to be real with her and tell her the truth, but too much time had passed, and there was no bridge between them, especially now that their children were gone.

"No, I'm fine," he said. How could he tell her that he was in love with a woman who had left him because he was married, who didn't want to be the cause of the demise of the marriage and didn't believe he would ever get divorced? And now that she was gone, he was even more aware of how nonexistent the marriage was. It had been on life support for so many years it was never going to regain consciousness. It had flatlined right from the beginning, and they should have pulled the plug then, even before they tried to breathe life into it by having children. He loved their sons, but they had only underlined the differences between him and Stephanie. And the chasm was too wide to bridge. He was almost ready to let go now, but he couldn't do it while she was sick. He wanted to wait to tell her until she recovered. It didn't seem fair to tell her before that. He owed her an easy convalescence at least. He was well aware now of how little he had contributed to her life, other than money. And that wasn't enough.

"You don't have to hang around for us, you know," she reminded him. "If there's something you want to do for yourself."

"Thank you," he said, touched that she had considered him. "I'm fine for now. And your friends run a pretty good restaurant. I'm going to get fat while you get well."

"Yeah, me too. Veronique is a cordon bleu chef." Stephanie could barely cook an egg and didn't care. "Lizzie is better in the saddle than in the kitchen. If you had to depend on us, you'd starve." He noticed, as he always did, how deep her affection was for her friends, more even than for him or their children. She had been lucky to find them over the years. Their bond was worth more than her marriage. And each of them brought something to the group. Together they made a solid whole. He and Stephanie had nothing that compared to it.

"Can I do anything for you? Anything you need?" he offered before he left for the day. She looked as though she were going to say something, but she didn't. She didn't want to contribute to what appeared to be a melancholy mood. He looked very down. She remembered him looking that way when they both figured out early on that they'd made a mistake. And yet they'd stayed, and trudged on. She could never have admitted it to her parents. It would have been the ultimate disgrace to admit that she'd married the wrong man, and even more so if she wanted out. They were an aristocratic Catholic family, and divorce was unimaginable. Now her parents were too far gone with Alzheimer's to know. And she and Olivier were still there. Having her three best friends made that mistake livable, and she wondered what he had to keep him going. She had sensed accurately that his new romance had come to an end, and she was sorry for him. She hoped he found someone else soon. She of all people knew that people weren't meant to live alone. It was feasible, but at a high price. She had done it herself until she met her "girls."

Olivier left for the office then, and Stephanie lay in bed, thinking, for a long time. She was sorry that she and Olivier weren't better friends and couldn't talk openly, and she was grateful that he didn't object to her close companions in the house. She would have been lost without them, and they were standing by her now, and so was he. She had to give him credit for that, and it surprised her. She had expected him to run for cover when she got hurt. Instead she felt a closeness to him, and a warmth she hadn't felt in years, and a deep compassion for him and how profoundly unhappy she could sense he was. And she felt sorrow for him over the person he seemed to have found briefly, and then lost. She probably wasn't the right one if it ended so quickly. Stephanie couldn't guess that she herself was the reason for it, and their marriage, even as nonexistent as it was.

Olivier waved to Lizzie as he drove away. She was skipping rope in the garden to keep in shape. She had an amazing body, but she felt like a sister to him now.

He had left several more messages for Amanda after Pascal had called him, but she didn't return the calls. She was true to herself and what she believed, and he was sure he wouldn't hear from her again, nor see her. She was gone for good. He just had to learn to live with it, like a severed limb. He couldn't replace her and didn't want to. She was unique.

Tom had called Amanda after his visit from the police and spoke to her in a growl. He called her at the gallery and used a menacing tone.

"How dare you say those things to the police about me? You tried to convince them that I broke into your apartment and tried to rape you."

"I didn't try to do anything, Tom. I raised the possibility about the apartment, and you lied to them about me and told them we were having an affair. What you did in the car after the movie was disgusting and unforgivable."

"You did it with that French bastard you were sleeping with. Why not with me? You led me on."

"No, I didn't. I made it clear to you right from the beginning when you got here that I only wanted to be friends. And whatever I did or didn't do, nothing justifies that kind of violence and abuse. You left me with bruises."

"I'm sorry," he said in a low voice, and for an instant she thought he was crying, but she wasn't sure. "I wanted you so badly, I lost control. I didn't mean to hurt you, Amanda. It won't happen again. And I would never break into your home. I don't climb through second-floor windows and destroy things. You know me better than that." It was what Pascal had said too. He was a monster to have brutalized her physically, but he wasn't crazy. He wouldn't climb up a building to steal her underwear and destroy her paintings. That was another person.

"Actually, I don't know you, Tom. The man you were that night is someone I don't know, and don't want to know."

"You drove me to it. You know I love you."

"That's not love, Tom. It's something very different." His rage had been terrifying.

"I'm sorry," he sounded contrite.

"Don't call me again," she said, and meant it, and then she hung up. She had nothing more to say to him.

He texted her seconds later. "You broke my heart again." As she read it, a distant memory came back to her, of when he had left NYU to attend Stanford. He desperately wanted her to continue the relationship with him long-distance, and she wouldn't. He had been weighing heavily on her for the past few months, and she didn't feel ready for the kind of commitment it would take to maintain a relationship with three thousand miles between them, and she had ended it when he left. She had spoken to her father about it before she did, and he agreed.

"If you don't feel ready, then don't do it. Be honest with him, that's always better. He's young. He'll get over it." Her father had been proud of her when she told him she had ended it cleanly. But she had forgotten that Tom had sent her anguished letters for a few months, begging her to reconsider. She wasn't dating anyone else yet, but she knew that it was over for her, and she didn't want to be tied to him. And he was so jealous, she knew he would be constantly accusing her of sleeping with other people, which she never did in the year they were together. In her entire life, she had never cheated on anyone.

The first few months with Tom had been blissful, but the last six months of their year together had been difficult, with a merry-go-round of accusations, arguments, and the silent treatment. It was a relief when he left. It would have been much harder if he stayed, so his transfer to Stanford had been providential, getting her out of the relationship simply and cleanly. It was only now that she recalled how insistent he had been, and eventually how nasty he had gotten when she refused to commit to him. Time had erased how unpleasant that had been for a while. And she assumed that they had all grown up. He had been married in the meantime, had a dignified career, was a respected attorney at an important firm, but deep inside he was still the angry, needy, rage-filled young man he'd been then, when he didn't get his way. She recalled that he had been abused by an alcoholic father as a boy, and that his mother had abandoned him and left with another man. Tom had anger issues that he had never resolved. They seemed to have gotten worse and Amanda felt sorry for the wife who had divorced him, although she'd stuck it out for fourteen years. Something about him was unstable, but she agreed with Pascal that he wasn't a burglar or a vandal, although he could have turned out to be a rapist if she hadn't run faster than he did. Whatever he was, she didn't want to see or hear from him again.

She told Pascal about the call and he was angry about it. "That bastard needs to leave you alone," he said emphatically.

"He swears he didn't break into the apartment."

"I believe him. I told you that myself. But that doesn't change the fact that he brutalized you and nearly raped you. And scared you to death. Some guys think they can do anything they want to women, either seduce them and convince them to sleep with them or punish them when they don't. And it was disgusting of him to lie to the police about you to discredit you and get himself off the hook. The guy is slime."

"He is. He wasn't that bad in college, but he is now. I think he has a lot of rage about his ex-wife, and his mother before that. She abandoned him when he was ten."

"That's not your problem. He needs therapy to work that out. You're not his therapist or his punching bag. And I can't believe you have two men like that at the moment. I don't think Quinlan will

come after you again, but the police still have to find your stalker."
Pascal didn't like the fact that it was taking them so long, but they
had warned her that it would. They had no idea who had broken
into her apartment. They had searched for fingerprints and had
found none. The police said that whoever had vandalized her apartment had worn gloves. He was no fool, and he had no desire to get
caught. It seemed like just a coincidence now that the stalker had
written the word "Bitch" on one of her paintings, which was what
Tom had called her when she didn't want to have sex with him and
he'd tried to force her.

She didn't hear from Tom after that, but she still got two or three
calls from a blocked number every night, which she didn't pick up.
She didn't want to change her number and lose real calls from
friends, so she just didn't answer the calls from blocked numbers at
night. The stalker never called her in the daytime, only very late at
night, and often woke her up. She guessed that he was hoping that
if he woke her, she'd be confused and pick up. She never did.

She couldn't wait for Tom to leave Paris and start his travels soon.
She didn't want to run into him anywhere, or have him show up at
the gallery or at home. She didn't think he would, but if he got
drunk some lonely night he might. The stalker was another story,
and special devices the police had recommended to prevent access
from her windows hadn't worked. The intruder had disabled them
with a hammer or some other instrument, and he had broken the
window and gone in. She had the alarm on at all times now, whenever she was home and when she went out.

And just in case Tom ever did show up and try to rape her again, before they disappeared completely, she took a selfie of the bruises on her breasts. They had faded a lot by then, but you could still see them.

It was a big day when Stephanie was finally well enough to visit the stables. Her friends drove her there. With her arm in a cast and the broken shoulder, she couldn't put a blouse or sweater on, so the nurse draped a blanket over her, and at the stable, she sat in the wheelchair with her leg in the cast, supported, resting and pointing straight out. It was a menace to pedestrians who didn't see her. The chair was heavy to maneuver, and even with one of her friends guiding it, they nearly knocked down several people on crowded sidewalks when they took her out. Lizzie was a menace with the wheelchair.

Stephanie felt as though she'd been reborn when she saw her horses, and her favorite mare came running up to her in the corral. She nuzzled Stephanie's face with her velvety nose and licked her cheeks. Stephanie could hardly wait to ride again. It brought tears to her friends' eyes to see her, not walking yet, but with her face lit up just being there. It had been Lizzie's idea to take her. Stephanie talked about her horses constantly, and Lizzie thought it would boost her spirits immeasurably. And it did. She was exhausted by the effort, but she looked like a new person after she met with one of her therapists and had Lizzie roll her into the kitchen to have dinner with the others.

Olivier looked shocked to see her there when he got home.

"Well, well, to what do we owe the honor?" He addressed his wife, and she grinned. She had come downstairs in the chair lift

Olivier had installed for her. It had worked well, and it had raised her spirits to be able to come to dinner with the others, instead of eating alone in her room on a tray.

"We went to the stables today. Tillie came galloping over and licked my face. She didn't leave me for a second until we had to go. I can't wait to go back."

Olivier smiled his approval and addressed the group. "Whose idea was that?"

"Lizzie's." Stephanie spoke up immediately, and Lizzie smiled up at him.

"Good job, Red." He teased her about her red hair now, and she always came up with the best ideas to boost Stephanie's spirits. He sat down and had dinner with them, helped them clean up, and then went to his bedroom to make some calls. He was in a pretty decent mood himself. His company had signed a big author that day whom they'd been pursuing for a year. It was a major victory for Olivier. It reminded him that he needed to get back to having lunches and dinners with his authors. He hadn't been since he and Amanda had broken up. He used Stephanie's accident as an excuse. He didn't have the heart to see anyone, not even the writers he loved.

After he went to his bedroom, Stephanie went back upstairs on the lift and they took the wheelchair up to her bedroom. She was still flying from her visit to the stables. Veronique and Valerie went back downstairs then to finish cleaning up the kitchen, and the nurse went to get Stephanie's meds for the night. Stephanie and Lizzie were alone in her bedroom then, and Lizzie looked like she had something on her mind. "Is something wrong?" Stephanie asked her, always concerned about her. Stephanie normally took the motherly role with Lizzie, but ever since the accident, Lizzie had been the chief caretaker and nurturer.

"No. I've been thinking ever since all this happened. I feel sorry for Olivier. He's a really nice guy, more than I realized before the accident. He doesn't know what to do to help you, or what to say, but he cares, and he tries all the time. He keeps trying to come up with therapies or massages or exercise programs that will get you well faster and make you feel better," Lizzie said gently.

"And so do you," Stephanie said gratefully.

"I know, but I'm not married to you, Steph. You always say your marriage has been dead for years, that it never should have happened. Are you sure? I feel like we're all getting in the way of your making it work with him again. Do you want us to go?" She looked heartbroken as she said it, and there were tears in her eyes.

"No, I don't," Stephanie said in a husky voice, and held Lizzie's hand. "It's too late for us, for me and Olivier. It's always been a mistake. My having the accident doesn't make the marriage viable again, it just gives us the chance to see what a nice man he is. But he's not 'my' nice man. He never was, and never could be. I need you here," she said as she held Lizzie's hand. "It's rotten of me to say, because he is a nice man, but I don't need him the way I need you."

"Do you think he wants you back, to make it work again?" Lizzie had begun to think so.

"No. And even if he did, it would be a disaster in five minutes. I think we both know that."

"You have kids together, and none of us have children or husbands, or family we're close to. I don't want to stand in the way, if that's what you want with him."

"It isn't. I couldn't do it, no matter how nice he is. We never had chemistry. I didn't have chemistry with him even in the beginning. I had no idea what that is. It's that ephemeral ingredient that makes a relationship work and gets you over the bumps. I thought chemistry was something that happened in the lab, or the classroom with a bottle of acid with a lot of smoke pouring out of it, like magic. Chemistry is magic. Olivier is a lovely man, but he never had that magical ingredient. You can't fake that, or invent it. We have great kids, but that's the only good thing we ever had. I don't want to go back to being his wife again in a real way. If I did, it would be a fraud. I did that for too long." Lizzie nodded and smiled at her, and reached over and hugged her, and then the nurse walked in with Stephanie's meds, and Lizzie went back downstairs to the others.

Chapter 14

Amanda had additional locks put on her windows, and new handhold barriers the police had recommended to make it impossible for someone to climb up the façade and get in through the windows. Her apartment was beginning to feel like a prison. And she slept with the alarm on, in case someone managed to scale the wall to her windows anyway. She had a hard time sleeping at night, feeling as though someone was watching her and waiting to invade her home again. It was a feeling of constant tension. And Pascal saw easily the toll it was taking on her. She was suddenly too thin and pale, and had dark circles under her eyes. On some days, she looked sick, although she insisted she was fine. Pascal could see that she wasn't.

"You need a break," he told her one morning when she looked particularly worn out. Even Lulu was looking tired. Amanda woke up several times a night now, checked the windows and doors, and then couldn't get back to sleep. Lulu followed her around dutifully,

203

and slept at the gallery all day to recover from the sleepless nights. "Why don't you go away for a weekend somewhere?"

"That's depressing on your own. It would make me feel like a loser," she said honestly. "Couples strolling down the beach, and me alone with Lulu under a parasol."

The image didn't appeal to Pascal either. He had spoken to Olivier a couple of times, who had reported that Amanda hadn't responded to a single one of his calls, or even text messages. She had closed the door firmly, and locked it. She was defending her home from stalkers and burglars, and her heart from Olivier. He had given up and stopped trying to reach her, and told Pascal it was hopeless. He had made up his mind to get divorced once Stephanie recovered, for his own sake, but he felt it was still too soon to tell her, so he was respectfully waiting until she was back on her feet. And there was no evidence of his decision yet for him to show Amanda, and he knew she wouldn't believe him.

"It's too depressing and bad for your health to sit in your apartment waiting for someone to scale the walls again," Pascal told Amanda. She had panic buttons now, connected directly to the police, and they had warnings on their dispatch computers to respond immediately if she hit the panic button she kept in her pocket whenever she was home. It was like living on a time bomb, waiting for something to happen. "I have an idea," Pascal said. "I never sleep at my apartment anymore. I'm always at Delphine's place. I just keep mine now in case something goes wrong with us." He had actually been faithful to his latest love for several months, a first for him. He had told Amanda several times that Delphine would probably kill him if he cheated on her. But the most shocking thing of all, from his point of view, was that he didn't want to. He wondered if it was due to age, or a sign of true love. He wasn't sure which.

"Why don't you stay at my apartment for a while, just for a change of scene, so you can sleep, and you don't have to spend the night with the panic button in your hand, waiting for someone to climb in the windows to steal your knickers or cut your couch in half?" She had ordered a new one from Italy, and they told her it would take six or eight months.

"I feel silly staying at your place. I should be able to stay at my own. It seems cowardly to run."

"It seems smart to me. At least for a while. Think about it." She promised to, but was inclined to dismiss it. But after another week of sleepless nights, she finally conceded.

"But just for a few days, or a week. I'm not going to move in and invade your space," she said. But the idea definitely had some appeal. Pascal lived in a rickety old-fashioned building on the Left Bank, but he had a beautiful sunny living room, a comfortable bedroom with a view of the Eiffel Tower, and a kitchen that belonged in a museum, but she didn't care since she couldn't cook.

Amanda packed a bag for the weekend, suddenly excited by the idea. She and Lulu moved in on Saturday morning, and she went to the flower market and brought back mountains of flowers and blossoming branches, filling all the vases Pascal had of various sizes, and his apartment looked like a garden in full bloom when she was finished. She bought some sausages and a bottle of her favorite white wine for dinner. She walked Lulu along the Seine that night, and felt safe for the first time in months when she went to bed. She slept for eleven hours, and went for a long walk in the Bois de Boulogne with

Lulu the next day. She went to check on her own apartment, and everything was fine. And after another long peaceful sleep that night, she arrived at the gallery Monday morning looking rejuvenated and like a new person, and she felt like one.

"Sleep is a miracle drug. Thank you for lending me the apartment," she said gratefully.

"Stay as long as you want," he said, pleased to see her looking better, without the dark circles under her eyes that had become all too familiar. Between Tom, Olivier, and her unidentified erotomaniac, too much had happened to her in too short a time. And living in her apartment, waiting to be attacked again, was just too stressful for her. Staying at Pascal's gave her a reprieve.

It felt like an adventure now going to his apartment every night, with the beautiful view, the open sky, the life of the river, the boats drifting by. It was a fresh view of Paris, which she enjoyed. She went back and forth to her own apartment daily to pick up her mail and fresh clothes. Her apartment had a slightly stale feeling to it, with the windows closed. She opened them when she came home, to let in some air, and then locked everything up again when she left. She didn't miss it yet. It was fun to have a change, second best to a vacation, and there were some things she wanted to change when she came back. She decided that she needed new kitchen curtains and a new rug in the front hall. The one she had had never fully recovered from the chemicals she and Olivier used to get rid of the fish blood when the stalker left her the florist box with the fish in it. She was going to look for a rug and fabric for the curtains the following weekend. She saw everything with a new eye since she wasn't there every day. Lulu always looked happy to come home and a little disappointed when they left, but Amanda brought her favorite bed to Pascal's, and a bag of her toys, and Lulu was happier after that.

Amanda had been at Pascal's for a week when they had a major rainstorm that lasted for three days. His apartment was on the sixth floor, just under the picturesque mansard roof. Two of the windows in the living room were the original eighteenth-century round ones, and leaked so badly there was water all over the floor when she got home. And there was a major leak over the bed which Pascal hadn't told her about. She used all her strength to move his antique iron bed, but the room wasn't big enough to move it completely out of the way of the leak, so rain dripped onto her face all night, and in the morning the lower half of the bed was soaking wet. The apartment had a huge amount of charm, but some noticeable flaws Pascal had failed to mention. She slept on the couch, but the wind whistled through the oeil-de-boeuf ("bull's eye") windows all night, and she was cold when she woke up. The weather had gotten chilly with the storm.

Everything in her own apartment was in impeccable condition and good repair. She owned hers and maintained it beautifully. He only rented his and the landlord couldn't afford to do repairs, and wasn't willing to. Pascal knew all about the leaks and apologized to Amanda. His furniture was ancient, and there was nothing of value there, so he didn't care. She knew the apartment was cold and drafty in winter too, and every winter Pascal threatened to give it up, but he loved it, so he never did. On the fourth night of driving rain, which loosened more tiles on the roof and caused more leaks, she went back to her own apartment at two A.M. It seemed better to be dry, even if a little less safe. She left her things at his place, and took a cab to her own apartment, and went back to Pascal's in the morning to collect her things. She had been there for eleven days, and it seemed long enough. She was less stressed when she went back to her apartment, and Lulu ran up and down the hall barking, happy to be home.

"Okay, okay, you snob." Amanda laughed at her, in much better spirits than when they'd left. She listed all the problems to Pascal when she saw him, and he was apologetic again.

"I'm sorry. I didn't think it would rain so much at this time of year. It's brutal in the winter, between the wind and the leaks. The landlord needs to redo all the windows and the roof, and he won't. I should probably give the place up. I guess I will if things work out with Delphine, and so far it's looking pretty good. Her place is really too small for the two of us, so we're talking about finding a new apartment together."

"That's good news. And I had fun being at your place." Amanda looked better than she had in a while, and more relaxed, and she had slept well in her own apartment for the past two nights. A little sleep had given her a new lease on life.

The rainy weather dampened everyone's mood at Olivier and Stephanie's house. They played Scrabble, dominoes, and cards for a few days. Valerie baked a delicious cake, and Veronique prepared a traditional cassoulet. They all worried about their horses not getting enough exercise in the rain, and Oliver seemed a little out of sorts when every room he walked into had one or several women in it, laughing, talking, eating, or playing games. He needed his own space, and couldn't find any anywhere. He went for a long walk in the rain, and came back soaked. And when it finally stopped, the Three Musketeers, as he called them, took a drive to check on their horses.

He waved to Stephanie as he walked past her bedroom, and saw that she was looking wistfully out the window, wishing she could join them. She was still in a wheelchair most of the time, but she longed to get up and walk, and she couldn't yet. She'd been waiting to talk to him all day, but she couldn't find a time when the others weren't with her. She turned to look at him with a serious face.

"Something wrong?" He hoped not. He wasn't in the mood to listen to anyone's complaints about the weather or the nurse. He felt like he was running a convalescent home for wayward women.

Stephanie didn't answer his question, which wasn't a good sign, and with a feeling of trepidation, he walked into the room. She looked up at him with serious eyes that were as stormy as the sky outside. "What's up?"

"Do you have a minute to talk?" She knew it wasn't a good time, but it was rare that all the others went out at the same time, and she didn't want to wait. She had been wanting to talk to him for weeks, and there would never be a good time for what she had to say.

"I guess so," he said, without much enthusiasm. His hair was still wet from the rain, and his boots were soaked.

"I have something to tell you," Stephanie said in a small voice, squeezing her hands together nervously. She looked like she was praying, and her eyes were sad and earnest when she brought them to his face. Olivier couldn't think of anything that could warrant that kind of solemnity and dreaded what she would say. The rain was depressing all of them, and she had been cooped up for a long time, and in pain. She was better now, but she still had a long way to go until she reached full recovery, and some days she was afraid she never would. He thought she was having a sinker now, and he wasn't in the mood to cheer her up, but he knew he'd have to. There was no one else around to do it. Lizzie was her morale booster, but she'd gone with the others.

"It can't be as bad as all that," he said, smiling at her.

"That depends on your point of view," Stephanie said. He suddenly wondered if she'd had bad medical news, and if she was sick, in some other very serious way.

"Are you okay?" he asked her, and she hesitated and then nodded.

"You've been incredibly good through this whole mess ever since the accident. I feel terrible that we've all imposed on you, and you must be sick of it by now. My horsey group, the nurses, me like a dead whale in bed most of the time or drugged out of my mind or asleep. It's a lot of people in the house, and neither of us is used to it, or to being here together anymore. I'm never here, you do what you want, and suddenly you're invaded by an army. I'm sorry and you've been wonderful about it."

"Is that all you wanted to say?" he asked, relieved.

"No, but I just want you to know how much I appreciate it before I say the rest." He could hear bells and alarms going off in his head. It sounded like the beginning of a conversation they had been avoiding for years. He guessed that she was going to either clip his wings or ask him things he didn't want to tell her.

"Before you start, are you sure you want to do this now?" he asked her. She looked quiet and calm when she nodded, and he was filled with dread. She was not going to be deterred.

"We have to talk about this, Olivier. We've been avoiding each other for years, I more than you. When the accident happened, I realized how little we know each other. We're strangers living in the same house. We always have been. I never knew you, or myself. We were children when we were married, and I think we both tried to make it work. And we both knew we'd made a terrible mistake. I thought you were the wrong man, and I was the wrong woman for you. My parents told me we had to stick with it, that they'd had a hard time at first too. So I listened to them, and I shouldn't have. I didn't know what was wrong. I talked to a priest, and he said a baby would fix everything. It didn't. It made it worse.

"And I thought something terrible was wrong with me. I didn't know how to be a mother, and didn't want to know, and you were mother and father to Guillaume. You actually did a very good job of it, and poor Edouard was just one more weight around our necks, but somehow he seems to have survived it and doesn't hate us, although he should hate me. I ran off with my horses, and the people I met. I've been doing it for more than twenty years and you never complain. I don't know why not. We could have gotten out of it, and we never did. We should have." Olivier had no idea where she was going, if she wanted out, or back in and a chance to start over and do it all again. He didn't want either. In theory, he wanted a divorce, but he had wanted it in order to be with Amanda, and she was gone, and he didn't want to rekindle anything with Stephanie. He didn't have those feelings for her and was sure he never would. He was still in love with Amanda, even though she was gone forever.

"It's too late now to think about what we should have done, Steph. The past is over, it's behind us. It is what it is now, and the real question is whether we want to live like this forever, or let it go. I've been thinking about it a lot myself." It was a relief when he said it to her, and easier than he thought it would be. Maybe they were ready.

"You have? I thought your latest romance was over," she said openly, and he decided to be honest with her.

"It is. But I don't want my life to be over, or to live dishonestly with you. I think that's where we went wrong."

"I've been dishonest with you since the day I married you," Stephanie said simply, and he stared at her, surprised.

"You have? How so? I thought I was the dishonest one here, and I feel guilty about it now. Once I thought we'd made an irreparable mistake, I never gave the marriage a chance again, and then you were gone anyway. So, I gave up. I've been playing at being your husband for years. We weren't even friends. I think we are now," which was what had made the conversation possible. They had never been this frank with each other, and suddenly he was glad she had started it. He hadn't had the courage to. And she was right. It was time.

"I had an experience when I was in boarding school," she admitted to him. "I thought it was a stupid one-time girl thing. I knew other girls who did too. I was sixteen. I put it out of my mind and went on. I never told anyone about it. And five years later, I married you. And I knew something was wrong with me. I didn't know what. I didn't have the guts to ask myself, but I knew. I knew it after Edouard was born. I was twenty-four years old. And I ran. I ran into my horse life. I created a world for myself where I could hide, from the truth and from you. And when I was twenty-seven, I fell in love, really in love for the first time. With Lizzie. And I'm still in love with her, and I hope I will be till my dying day. I cheated you, not just cheated *on* you. I cheated you of the opportunity to have a real life, to meet the right person, someone who could love you, and not run away from you and shrink from your touch. I don't know if you ever found someone you cared about. Your romances always seemed to be fleeting. I always thought you'd want a divorce eventually, but you didn't. I forced you to live this lie with me, which cheated you of the chance to find what I did with Lizzie. She was only eighteen then, and I was nine years older. I couldn't face the shock it would be to our families and to you. But I don't want to live a lie anymore. This is going to be hard for the boys, and for you, but I have to do it. I owe Lizzie that, I owe myself that, and I owe you that." She sat waiting for the roof to fall in and it didn't. She waited for Olivier to be furious with her, and he wasn't. He was stunned.

"Have you always known that you preferred women, or only wanted women?" he asked her, and she nodded.

"I think so now. I just didn't want to face it. Once I met Lizzie, I had to. Before that, I told myself that it was something I did for fun sometimes, or I'd had too much wine, or other people did it too. I never faced that it was what I wanted and who I was, who I am, and more and more so as the years went by. I don't want to play that game anymore, and lie, and especially not to you. You don't deserve that. I should have told you the truth right at the beginning, or at least twenty years ago, once I was sure. With my whole heart, Olivier, I apologize to you, for all the lies I told you, for the lie I forced you to live." He smiled at what she said and took her hand and held it.

"I told you my share of lies too." He wondered then. "What about the others? Are they gay too?" She nodded, about her friends.

"Veronique and Valerie are a couple. They were married to men, and both got divorced to be together. Lizzie is the brave one in the group. She told her parents when she was seventeen that she was sure. They're a very traditional family, ardently Catholic, both her uncles are bishops. Her family disowned her and have never seen her since. She paid a high price for her honesty. She's a brave girl. I've been supporting her for years on the money my parents left me. I lied to you about that too. I even bought her horses. She's a very reasonable, responsible person, and she was even at eighteen. And very discreet. I even thought of adopting her, but it was too big a lie, even for me. To tell you the whole story, I want a divorce. And now that the laws have changed, I want to marry Lizzie." Olivier was dead silent for a minute, digesting what she had said to him. It was enormous, and she knew it. In half an hour, he had gone from being a man with a wife, even if their marriage was rocky, to discovering that the whole twenty-six years of their married life had been a lie and she wanted a divorce and was going to marry a woman. It was a lot to swallow. He was still holding her hand.

"Thank you for being honest with me," he said, deeply moved.

"I had to be. You've been so good to me ever since I got hurt. It reminded me of who you are and what I owe you, and I do love you, just not as your wife. You don't deserve another twenty-six years of lies from me. And Lizzie felt wrong about it too. She loves you. She talked to me about it. She's noticed everything you've been doing for me and is grateful to you, and so am I."

"I love her too. What exactly will that make us now, Lizzie and me? My sister-in-law? My niece? My ex-wife's wife? My sons' aunt?"

he said in a teasing tone. Stephanie smiled at the irony of it and they both laughed. "Do I give you away at the wedding? It would shock the hell out of everyone we know, but oddly, I think I'd like that. It's very symbolic." And then he grew serious again. "We have to handle this well with the boys. I need to think about that."

"Me too," she agreed, amazed at how good he was being about it, which didn't totally surprise her. He was a good person, through and through, and the affairs he'd had had probably kept him going emotionally, from one fling to another, desperate for some form of affection, with a wife who gave him none at all. She thought his affairs had been justified and didn't blame him for them. She never had.

"I want a divorce too," he admitted to her. "I was going to talk to you about it when you were better. I thought it was too soon. I just lost a woman I really love because she didn't want to be with a married man. She thought that if she bowed out, you and I could rekindle our marriage. I told her I didn't think it was possible."

"You were right about that," Stephanie confirmed.

"She didn't believe me, so she ended it."

"I thought something like that had happened. You've been looking miserable."

He nodded. "I've been miserable."

"This ought to change things for her," Stephanie said quietly.

"She won't speak to me or return my calls or answer anything I write to her. I think she's over it."

"If she's a good person, she'll listen to you. Is she a good person?"

Stephanie felt protective of him now. He was no longer her enemy or her jailer. They could be friends and allies now.

"She's a very good person. That's why she left me. Out of respect for you and our marriage."

"Talk to her. This should make a big difference." He nodded, thinking about Amanda. "How old is she?"

"Thirty-nine, a year older than Lizzie. Almost forty in her case." They both sat, thinking for a minute. They had come far in the last hour and a half, and covered a lifetime, with all its truths and lies. They both felt lighter. Stephanie knew exactly where she was going now. She was lucky. And Olivier had taken it well, like the good man he was. But he didn't know where he was going. He didn't know if this would make a difference to Amanda. Maybe she had gone too far by now to come back to him. He recognized it as a possibility.

"I hope she comes back to you," Stephanie said softly.

"So do I," he said, looking at the woman who had been his wife for more than half his lifetime, and no longer wanted to be. They had been husband and wife, and now they were friends. They sat holding hands, as they heard the front door close and the others come in, back from the stables. He felt like part of their secret world now. "We'll have to work out the details later," he said to Stephanie in a low voice. "What we do with the house, where you're going to live."

"I think we should sell it. We don't need this house anymore. Lizzie and I want to get a small apartment where we can stay between shows, with room for the boys, of course."

"I was thinking along those lines too," he admitted, as Lizzie walked into the room and saw them holding hands. Her face went pale and grew instantly serious as Stephanie smiled at her from her wheelchair, and Olivier stood up, patted Lizzie's shoulder, and left to go to his own room, so Stephanie could talk to Lizzie and tell her the news.

Olivier sat down on his bed when he got to his room. His head was spinning and felt like it was going to explode. He wondered why he had never suspected the truth about Stephanie. She had covered it well, but he had lived with her for twenty-six years and it had never occurred to him. Her parents would have been devastated, but they were too far gone now to know or care, and it all made sense. And Lizzie was a good person. She and Stephanie had already withstood the test of time with each other. And now they could enjoy the rest of it together, without lying and hiding. He suspected that his sons would be shocked at first, but they might not be. Theirs was an entirely different generation with different views of what the norms were. Olivier's world would be shocked, but he didn't care. And Stephanie's world wouldn't be. She had built her parallel life well, and the people in her world would embrace her with open arms and celebrate her. He was impressed by how brave she was, and how brave she had just been with him. More than ever, he respected and admired the woman he had married, and he actually loved her. It hadn't been an entirely loveless marriage after all.

As soon as Olivier left the room, after patting Lizzie's shoulder, she looked at Stephanie with terror in her eyes. She had seen them holding hands when she came through the doorway, before he stood up. She approached Stephanie with caution, bracing for bad news.

"What just happened while we were out? Are you going to stay with him?" Stephanie had recently promised her she would ask him for a divorce at the right time.

"No. I told him about us. I told him the truth about all of it, all the way back to the beginning."

"What did he say?" Lizzie sank slowly into the chair Olivier had been sitting in.

"He was wonderful. He's probably the best man I'll ever know. We wasted a ridiculous number of years lying to each other and ourselves. And I wasted years for you and me too."

"You didn't waste them. We've been together all this time. You really only lied to him."

"And our boys. He was terrific about it. It made everything make sense to him." Stephanie smiled at Lizzie then. It had been an emotional afternoon. "He wants to give me away at our wedding. Or both of us, if you want." Lizzie was suddenly beaming as tears spilled down her cheeks. She had waited twenty years for this, since she was a teenager. Her parents had never forgiven her, but Stephanie had been everything to her. Mother, sister, lover, friend, and even mentor. Stephanie had been her whole world, and now they could come out of the shadows into the light of day.

"He's in love with someone too. It's not working out for the moment, but maybe he can get her back now. She left him because he's married. He won't be for long. I'll get things started now. I'll call the lawyer on Monday." Lizzie leaned close to Stephanie and put her head on her shoulder, and Stephanie put an arm around her. "I told you it would work out in the end." Lizzie had been worried.

"What made you tell him today?" she asked her.

"I have no idea. It just felt like the right time, and it was. How were the horses?"

"Restless. Bored. Like the rest of us." Lizzie glanced out the window into the garden as she said it, and smiled. She rushed to push Stephanie's wheelchair to the window, and there over the Paris sky was the biggest rainbow they had ever seen. "It's a sign," she said breathlessly, as Stephanie smiled at her, pulled her gently into the wheelchair with her, and kissed her.

Chapter 15

Olivier went for another walk after his long conversation with Stephanie. The rain had stopped and he needed some air. He was smiling as he walked along and saw the rainbow overhead. Stephanie had answered all his questions and explained everything. Their entire history made sense to him now. And what he wanted to do next was tell Amanda. Stephanie had taken the decision out of his hands and given him an immeasurable gift: an honest future to make up for their dishonest past. He only wished now that they had done it sooner.

He called Amanda from his cellphone while he was walking. It went straight to voicemail, and he left her a message that he had something urgent to tell her. In view of recent history, he doubted that she'd call him. He tried her again on the way back to the house, and texted her when he got home. Veronique was cooking dinner, and there was a celebratory atmosphere. Lizzie had told the others what had happened. All three of them smiled at Olivier, and he waved, as he headed up the stairs to his bedroom and called Amanda again. He sent her an email and said he needed to speak to her urgently. He had a feeling that nothing he said or wrote to her would induce her to call him. He had left her alone for a few weeks after pelting her with messages before that. Nothing had persuaded her to call him. She was determined to stay on her path and ignore him, and had shut him out.

Olivier was excited and wanted to share all the news with her. After he sent the email, he decided not to wait for a response but to go to her house and tell her. It was the only way he would get her to listen.

He told Stephanie he was going out, mostly out of habit, and she could guess where he was going. She called out to him as he rushed down the stairs.

"Good luck!"

"Thank you!" he shouted back, and poked his head into the kitchen. "I'm out for dinner, I think," he said to the Three Musketeers with a grin. "Leave me some leftovers just in case. It smells delicious." He realized that he was going to miss them when they left, once Stephanie was walking again. He'd miss her too, after more than half a lifetime with her, even though they didn't see each other often. But there would be holidays and family events with the boys, and he didn't see why they couldn't still spend them together. And Lizzie was always with them anyway.

He drove his car out of the garage and headed toward Amanda's apartment. She might be out, or refuse to let him in, but he had to try. Otherwise, he would have Pascal call her and tell her he was getting divorced, but he wanted to give her the news himself, if he could gain access to her, which wasn't a sure thing.

He parked half a block away from her building. It was the only spot he could find. It was already dark, and as he approached the building, he saw a shadow move on the façade. He stopped to look more carefully and realized it wasn't a shadow, it was a man, in black pants and a black sweater, a knitted hood and mask and black gloves. Not an inch of flesh was showing as he carefully made his way up the façade using the hand- and footholds that had been used before. Olivier couldn't see who the man was, but he was agile and scaling the building quickly. Olivier paused to look where he would stop, as he got a grip on Amanda's balcony, and leapt easily onto it. He was holding something that he used to smash the window. All her lights were on, so Olivier assumed that she was home.

Olivier didn't waste any time as he rushed at the front door with the code panel. He pressed all the correct numbers and it opened, and he raced up the stairs, taking them two at a time at full speed while calling the police on his cellphone. They answered immediately and he told them where he was, Amanda's name, and what was happening. His stomach turned over as he backed up to kick in her apartment door. He didn't have a key, and there was no other way to get in.

Amanda was in a pink terry-cloth robe tied tightly around her as she walked into her bedroom, her hair wet. She hadn't set the alarm yet for the night, and she was beginning to feel safe in her apartment again. She'd been in the shower when the intruder broke the window, climbed in, and took his hat and mask off. He was waiting for her in the middle of the bedroom, as Amanda saw him and gave a start. It was Tom.

"What are you doing here? How did you get in?" she said, shaking and trying not to show it, as he walked slowly toward her, his face contorted by rage. Lulu was barking frantically at him and he paid no attention to her.

"I wasn't good enough for you, Amanda, was I? But he was. I know what you did with him. I saw how often he was here. You're a whore, that's all you are. I know how many nights he slept here." He advanced on her as she backed away. She felt in the pocket of her robe for the panic button but it was behind him on the dresser and she couldn't get to it. She wanted to run into her bathroom and lock the door, but it would mean leaving Lulu with him, and she was afraid he would kill the dog. And as she thought it, he pulled a long switchblade out of his pocket and flashed it at Amanda. "Remember how the book ends, and what happens to the girl he loved. He kills her. Just like I'm going to kill you now. But first I'm going to show you what love feels like." He put the switchblade back in his pocket, took another step toward her, and slapped her hard across the face. She could taste blood when he did, and with a single gesture he untied her robe, and with two hands threw her on the bed and climbed on top of her with his full weight, fully intending to rape her. She was lying naked beneath him, trying to fight him off with her legs and feet as he pinned her arms down with his hands. He reached down to push his pants down, and as he did there was a crashing sound, and suddenly two powerful arms and a towering figure pulled him off her, and he flew backward. Amanda saw Olivier's face as he knocked Tom down, and faster than light, Tom was on his feet again, with the blade of his switchblade flashing. Olivier had a grip on him, and Tom slashed at his arm to free himself, and suddenly there was blood everywhere, and at lightning speed, Tom turned and lunged at Amanda to slash her, and his blade cut into her thigh. Olivier grabbed Tom and knocked him to the floor then, pinning him down with his full weight as four police officers ran through her open front door and into her bedroom with guns drawn and took over. In less than a minute they had Tom in handcuffs down on the floor with his arms behind him. He was shouting obscenities at Olivier and Amanda and trying to kick the police officers, who tied his legs together so he couldn't move. There was a pool of blood on Amanda's bedroom floor, as she stood naked with blood gushing from her thigh. One of the officers covered her with her robe and sat her on the bed, as two others tended to Olivier. His shirt drenched in blood, he was still conscious, talking to the police. Tom had cut his arm but not his chest. And Lulu was cowering in the corner, whimpering, as the fourth officer called for emergency medical services, the SAMU.

Tom rolled so he could see Amanda, sitting on the bed in shock, and shouted at her. "I should have killed you. You're a bitch! You always were. You deserve to die!" His words were so venomous and his face so contorted with fury that she almost didn't recognize him. He had cut his arm when he broke the window, and he was bleeding too. It was a scene of carnage in her bedroom.

Olivier looked over at Amanda and saw her bleeding on the bed, her legs covered in blood, her robe and his shirt drenched with it.

"Are you okay?" he asked her in a weak voice, and she nodded, too traumatized to speak, and within minutes, the room was filled with the emergency medical teams. Tom had been removed, and they put Olivier and Amanda on two gurneys and carried them downstairs to the ambulance. The street was full of police cars and flashing lights. Amanda asked about her dog, and one of the officers said she was fine, and they had left her in the kitchen of the apartment and locked the door. And then they closed the ambulance doors and sped away to the Pitié-Salpêtrière Hospital, taking them both to the trauma unit to be assessed for their injuries. Tom had been taken straight to jail, and if he needed stitches for the cuts on his hands from the broken window, they would stitch him up there.

The doctors were applying pressure to Olivier's arm while they examined him, and a detective was asking him questions. He had an IV in his other arm, and he kept looking over at Amanda and asking if she was okay.

They stitched them up and gave them tetanus shots, assessing their injuries as deep flesh wounds. Olivier and Amanda both required stitches but no nerves or ligaments had been cut, no arteries had been hit. They were told that they were very lucky.

The detective questioned Amanda too, and she gave him all the background. It was clear now that Tom had been her erotomaniac all along, and had also done the first two break-ins since they were identical in style. And he had probably left the gutted fish in the florist box.

They kept Amanda and Olivier for observation overnight, until nine o'clock the next morning, and two police officers took them back to her apartment in a police car. The nurses gave them hospital pajamas to go home in. Amanda had no clothes with her, and Olivier's were cut from the switchblade and covered in blood, and had been taken into evidence. Amanda and Olivier were told there would be no lasting damage from their injuries. Their wounds had bled a lot, but there was no significant blood loss that required transfusions.

The detective who had questioned Amanda told her that Olivier had saved her. If he hadn't called the police and broken the door down before they got there, Tom would have raped and killed her. He had admitted as much to the police and said she deserved it.

The police had locked the door to the apartment when they left, and they got the key from the guardian when they returned. They walked Olivier and Amanda into the apartment, brought them each a glass of water, pulled the blood-soaked sheets off the bed and let them lie down, and then freed Lulu from the kitchen. She immediately came to find Amanda, who picked her up, and Lulu licked her face, happy to see her. Before they left, the police officers made sure that Amanda and Olivier were doing all right, and informed them that a criminal investigation unit would come by to see them that afternoon with further questions and information, and that a follow-up medical team would come to check their wounds. And then the officers left.

Olivier and Amanda lay on her bed with a blanket over them, with the broken window, and felt like they had been washed up on the beach after a shipwreck. And Lulu lay next to her.

"Wow, how did all that happen?" Amanda asked Olivier. He wanted to put an arm around her, but he couldn't, since his left arm was bandaged and in a sling. "I came out of the bathroom and there he was, dressed like a cat burglar, and he slapped me and grabbed me. He was going to rape me. And then kill me. And what were you doing here?" They were both pale, but fully aware of what had happened and how fortunate they were that Tom hadn't killed them both.

"I came to tell you that I'm getting divorced, since you didn't answer any of my texts or messages, and when I got here I saw him crawling up the building and climbing onto your balcony. I could guess the rest. I called the police while I rushed up the stairs and kicked in the apartment door when he was about to rape you."

"He really is insane," Amanda said in an awestruck voice. "He was my stalker all along. And I don't think he found me by accident. I think he came to Paris looking for me, to settle an old score, for ending it with him twenty years ago."

"That's a horrifying thought," Olivier said, still feeling weak. It had been a shocking night.

"Why did you tell your wife you wanted a divorce?" she asked him. "Did you tell her about me?"

"I didn't, and yes, in that order. I was waiting until she had recovered from her accident, but she told me she was divorcing me. She explained twenty-six years to me in less than two hours. She agrees that we should have divorced years ago. She's gay, and she's been in love with one of her riding partners for twenty years, but she knew before that, before she even married me. She just never told me, or her family. The riding partner is a really lovely woman. They're getting married. And after that, I told Stephanie about you." Amanda was lying on her side on the bloodstained mattress and staring at him.

"Oh my God, what did you say to her when she told you?"

"I was grateful. It explained everything. She doesn't want to live a lie anymore, and neither do I. I would have asked her for a divorce in a month or two anyway. You'll never know how much I missed you."

"I missed you too," she said softly. "How did this craziness ever happen with Tom Quinlan?"

"There are some bad people out there," he said, and touched her with his good arm. Her leg was throbbing but she didn't care. Olivier was back, and he had saved her.

He lifted Lulu up with his good hand, and placed her between them, whimpering, as Amanda stroked her, and Olivier leaned toward Amanda and kissed her.

"What do you think will happen to Tom now?" she asked him as they lay there, catching up on everything they'd missed and the highlights of the last twenty-four hours, which were life-altering.

"He'll probably be charged with two counts of attempted murder and serve time in France. They don't extradite to the U.S. here. He looked like such a nice, normal guy."

They lay on the bed together for a while, thinking about all of it, and she called Pascal and told him what had happened. He was horrified.

"Oh my God, are you two okay? Why aren't you in the hospital?"

"They stitched us up and let us go this morning. They're coming to check on us later. We're all right, just kind of shell-shocked."

"Do you have food there?"

"I can't remember," she said, and Olivier laughed. Her domestic skills had not improved in his absence.

"Can we come over? I'll bring you something to eat." Pascal showed up half an hour later with Delphine and they brought crepes, omelets, pizza with an egg on it, some bread and cheese, and two steaming cups of cappuccino. Olivier ate as though he'd never seen food before, and Amanda ate the crepes and the omelet, and drank the cappuccino. Delphine had nearly fainted when she saw the blood on the rug and the mattress. Olivier and Amanda were still feeling shaky, but better after they ate. They sat at the kitchen table in their hospital pajamas and put the puzzle pieces together again for Pascal and Delphine. There were still things they didn't know, but they knew more than they did before. Tom was obviously psychotic and a potential killer. It reminded her of the end of the book he had described to her that he was so pleased with, where the hero kills the woman he loves. It had been a preview of things to come, and she didn't know it. She didn't realize then that the message and the ending were meant for her.

Pascal and Delphine stayed with Amanda and Olivier until the police detectives arrived to question them further. They had new information from Interpol, some of which Tom had admitted to them himself. The detectives' assessment was that he was deeply psychotic. He wasn't on sabbatical, and he was no longer a partner in the law firm. He had attacked his wife with a knife in a jealous rage and had been committed for a year to a hospital for the criminally insane. He was convicted of a felony, so he was disbarred, and had recently been released from the psychiatric hospital. He had admitted to the police that he had come to Paris to find Amanda because his wife was divorcing him. And he had started stalking her when he saw her with Olivier. He had broken into her apartment twice, the night before being the third time, and he intended to kill her then, after he raped her, and he said she deserved it. And Olivier had ruined everything. Tom was going to be charged with two counts of attempted murder and one of attempted rape and go to prison. And the police assured them both that he would serve a very long sentence in France. He was showing no remorse for what he'd done, and only expressed regret that he hadn't killed them both. It made Amanda shudder just hearing about it. But she was safe now. Her stalker had been apprehended. He couldn't hurt her again.

She and Olivier signed their statements, and the police thanked them and left. The medical team came shortly after and checked their dressings and their vital signs, were satisfied with their condition, and promised to come again the next day. Not surprisingly, they found that Amanda's heart rate was rapid, and Olivier's blood pressure was low from shock and loss of blood, but they were in surprisingly good condition given what they'd been through.

Amanda covered the mattress in towels after that, and made the bed with clean sheets. She was going to order a new mattress the next day, but they had to make do with it for tonight. She was going to try to have the rug cleaned. It was an antique Aubusson, and she wasn't sure they could save it. It seemed unimportant compared with all the rest. She and Olivier had survived, which was all that mattered.

Olivier called Stephanie to let her know that he was all right. He didn't want to worry her, so he didn't tell her what had happened or where he'd been.

"Did you get in touch with your friend?" she asked him.

He smiled when he answered. "I did."

"Was she pleased with the news?" He smiled at Amanda as he answered.

"I think so."

Pascal called later to check on them, and sent them dinner. He was so grateful they hadn't been killed.

Amanda and Olivier lay in bed together that night, thinking back on everything that had happened. She wondered if Tom had even written a book. Maybe all he'd done was plot to kill her, and nothing else.

It took Amanda and Olivier several days to recover from the trauma they'd been through, and to start to make plans for the future. They had a future now, and a life, which seemed infinitely precious. More than ever before.

"Do you want to move in with me?" Amanda asked him after he discussed the details of his divorce with her. They were going to sell the house, once Stephanie was fully recovered. She didn't want to be disturbed by potential buyers until she was well.

"Do you have room for me, like enough closet space?" Olivier asked her. She had only given him a very small closet before.

"No," she said cheerfully. "But I can make some."

"I'd like that," he said quietly, grateful for every moment with her. Stephanie's revelations had taught him how little one knew about people sometimes, even those you knew well. But nothing he had seen of Amanda worried him or made him feel uneasy.

Tom Quinlan signed a full confession and was sent to prison. He got life imprisonment for two counts of murder, since attempted murder carried the same weight in France. The attempted rape was added as an aggravating circumstance. And the attempt to murder Amanda was premeditated. His attorney estimated that he would serve twenty-five to thirty years. Twenty if he was exceptionally lucky, to be decided by a committee in later years. Olivier told Stephanie the story and she was shocked, and so relieved that he hadn't been killed.

It was another month before Stephanie was out of the wheelchair and on crutches. And at the end of another month, she was riding again. She wasn't ready for the shows yet, but Valerie, Veronique, and Lizzie had signed up for several and she was going to travel with them until she was fully recovered.

Before the four women left on the show circuit, they all had dinner together, with Olivier and Amanda. She told Stephanie about meeting her and Lizzie at the Hermès show, and Stephanie remembered.

Their divorce had already been filed, and Olivier and Stephanie had told their sons about it. They weren't surprised, and Stephanie had not told them yet about Lizzie. She was planning to in the coming months, and wanted to give them one big piece of news at a time. But both sons had said that their parents hadn't gotten along for all of their lives and hardly saw each other, so it wouldn't be a big change. Their mother marrying a woman would be a much bigger one. Amanda had a feeling they'd get through it, and Olivier was going to make it clear to them that he supported it, and thought their mother was very brave to be so honest. They still had to meet Amanda too, which compared to the rest would be a nonevent.

* * *

"Things move fast in your life," Pascal commented when Amanda talked to him about it. He was mildly surprised when she told him about Stephanie and the reason for the divorce, but they agreed that life was like that, full of surprises that no one could ever have predicted, and Stephanie and Olivier would set the tone, which hopefully would make it easier for their sons to accept.

The divorce was final in eight months, because there were no points of contention. Olivier and Stephanie agreed to an amicable settlement. They were going to divide the proceeds of the house sale in half, and Stephanie only wanted a very small spousal support to help defray the cost of the upkeep of her horses, which Olivier was happy to pay. They were fair with each other in the end, even if they had gotten off on the wrong foot at the start. They had been too young to know how to deal with the hand they'd been dealt. Stephanie had to come to terms with who she was, and Olivier had to be brave enough to want more out of life than he was getting. Amanda had shown him that. And in the end, Stephanie and Olivier had wound up with the right partners for them.

Amanda and Olivier went to Deauville and saw Stephanie ride in her first jumping competition when she was fully recovered. She won first place. She was back!

By the time the divorce was final, Guillaume and Edouard had been told about their mother and Lizzie. She chose the Christmas holidays to tell them, which wouldn't have been Olivier's first choice, but it was Stephanie's decision. Guillaume took it better than Edouard, who was more traditional, but in the end they agreed that it was their mother's life and her right to make the choices that suited her. And fortunately, they already knew Lizzie well and liked her a lot.

Amanda was easy for them when they met her. She brought no baggage to the table, and didn't interfere with their time with their father. She and Olivier took them on a skiing holiday in Verbier and spent the whole time enjoying each other and seeing friends. Amanda met the men at the bottom of the ski slope every day in her perfect après-ski outfits. Olivier was thrilled to see her. And she was easy and relaxed with his sons, who found her easy to relate to.

Amanda was young enough to be fun for them, and old enough to handle their family situation and complications with poise and delicacy. She was there to make things easier for Olivier, not more difficult. She made few demands on him. She was exactly what she had appeared to be from the beginning, an independent woman with a fine mind and a big heart, who loved him. He had everything with her that he'd always hoped for and never had, and she provided a warm home for him and his sons, which was more traditional than the scenario provided by their mother, who was happier now, at ease in her own skin, and better able to love them as a result.

Chapter 16

It was a beautiful balmy June day at the chic, perfectly tended, very social Paris Polo Club. It was where all the polo games were held, and Olivier's son Guillaume played there often when he was in Paris. The boys had grown up there, and it held warm memories for them. Their mother had carefully chosen the location.

There were eighty places set in the clubhouse restaurant, which had been taken over for the private event. Women in elegant hats arrived, mostly from Stephanie's riding club. Her parents would have approved of the choice of venue, or their chateau outside Paris, but the Polo Club was chic and fun, and very exclusive.

A makeshift altar had been set up with a lavish arch of white flowers, mostly orchids and lilies and white roses, with sprays of lily of the valley, and the arrangements on each table matched it. The crystal and silver gleamed, and the polo field was quiet. The officiant was a minister from the American Church in Paris. Stephanie had had a Catholic church wedding the first time, and was divorced, not annulled, so they needed a Protestant minister this time, and one who was comfortable marrying them.

Guillaume and Edouard were their witnesses and were honored to be asked. They stood tall in dark gray suits, their hair a little longer than their father would have liked, but looking neat and proper with shined shoes, new white shirts, and blue ties from Hermès.

Olivier walked the brides down the aisle, with one on either arm. The brides were both wearing white Chanel dresses. Stephanie's was a very simple white lace suit with an ankle-length skirt, and matching shoes, and Lizzie's was a short white satin jacket with a white tulle skirt that made her look very young and like a Degas ballerina. She had toned down her usual stilettoes for white satin ballerina flats in honor of the grass in the ceremony area. Olivier led them to the waiting minister and left them with him under the white floral arch. Both women were wearing short white veils and carrying bouquets of lily of the valley. It was a very proper wedding, with traditional vows. Everything about it respected time-honored customs familiar to all. The only thing missing was a groom, but no one seemed to mind.

And once he had left the brides at the altar, Olivier took his place in the front row next to his wife, Amanda, who was three months pregnant, a surprise baby having been conceived on their wedding night. It didn't show yet, and they were hoping for a girl, due in December. They had gotten married as soon as the divorce was final. Stephanie and Lizzie had waited a little longer, to fit the wedding into their show schedule.

The ceremony was solemn and respectful, the text only slightly adjusted for the circumstances and the homily a serious one. The brides walked down the grassy aisle after the ceremony, beaming, holding hands, wearing narrow gold wedding rings from Cartier. There had been no engagement rings. Their engagement had lasted twenty years and had already withstood the test of time.

The reception was jubilant, the champagne flowed, the music was joyous, there was dancing, and Olivier led his wife onto the dance floor with their baby between them. She had worn a pale blue dress with a matching hat and coat from Dior, and she looked radiant. They danced a slow waltz halfway through the afternoon and smiled.

"Happy?" he asked her.

"Perfectly. Exquisitely." And then she whispered to him. "Our wedding was more fun." They had been married at the American Cathedral Church of the Holy Trinity on the Avenue George V in Paris, by the same minister. Their reception for a hundred and fifty with a black-tie dinner was held at her gallery, and the guests danced all night to a band flown in from London, and a DJ that followed them. The wedding had been more formal and very elegant, and it suited them. Pascal had been best man, and did double duty and walked Amanda down the aisle. Stephanie's was more serious, to balance the social shockwaves caused by the fact that she was marrying a woman. Edouard and Guillaume were at both weddings, and were happy for their parents.

Olivier smiled as he looked at Amanda. "If anyone had told me twenty-six years ago that I'd be dancing at this wedding today, I'd have laughed at them."

"It's a pretty wedding, though, the girls did a nice job." Veronique and Valerie were the matrons of honor and had guided the caterer with an iron hand. Each of the two weddings was perfect for the people getting married.

"And now a new baby," he reminded her, and she blushed. Amanda was still embarrassed about being pregnant at forty.

"People will think I'm her grandmother," and she could have been, but in her heart she was still a young mother, and a bride three months earlier.

"It shows how unexpected life is. You never know what's going to happen, or who it will happen with. When I met you at that boring dinner party with the accordion that we both hated, who knew that I would marry you, or that I'd be standing here at my ex-wife's wedding to a woman. It's what makes life interesting," Olivier said. And no one who saw any of them would guess what they'd been through, the changes, the terrors, the heartbreaks, the disappointments, the joys, the things that seemed so important when they happened and were forgotten a few years later.

All that mattered was what was happening in that moment, that one shining instant when two people were joined in a private union shared with close friends who were there to support them, whether two women were marrying, or a man and a woman. They were two hearts fluttering through the stormy skies of real life, looking for the rainbow at the other end. Stephanie and Lizzie and Olivier and Amanda had found it. It was everything one could ask or hope for. They had found the right path for them, and the right person. And what anyone else thought of it didn't matter at all.

About the Author

DANIELLE STEEL has been hailed as one of the world's best-selling authors, with a billion copies of her novels sold. Her many international bestsellers include *Joy, Resurrection, Only the Brave, Never Too Late, Upside Down, The Ball at Versailles, Second Act, Happiness,* and other highly acclaimed novels. She is also the author of *His Bright Light,* the story of her son Nick Traina's life and death; *A Gift of Hope,* a memoir of her work with the homeless; *Expect a Miracle,* a book of her favorite quotations for inspiration and comfort; *Pure Joy,* about the dogs she and her family have loved; and the children's books *Pretty Minnie in Paris* and *Pretty Minnie in Hollywood.*

daniellesteel.com

Facebook.com/DanielleSteelOfficial

X: @daniellesteel

Instagram: @officialdaniellesteel

About the Type

This book was set in Charter, a typeface designed in 1987 by Matthew Carter (b. 1937) for Bitstream, Inc., a digital type-foundry that he cofounded in 1981. One of the most influential typographers of our time, Carter designed this versatile font to feature a compact width, squared serifs, and open letterforms. These features give the typeface a fresh, highly legible, and unencumbered appearance.